THE RED SEVEN

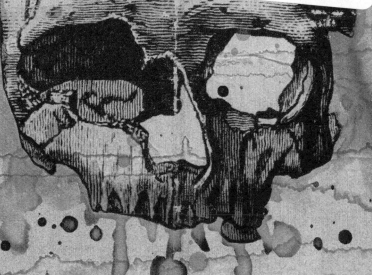

ROBERT DEAN

First Edition Trade Paperback

THE RED SEVEN © 2016 by Robert Dean
Cover art © 2016 by Matthew Revert
matthewrevert.com

This edition © 2016
Weird West Books (an imprint of Necro Publications)

ISBN: 978-1-944703-02-8
LOC: 2016931148

Assistant Editors:
Amanda Baird

Book design & typesetting:
David G. Barnett
Fat Cat Graphic Design
fatcatgraphicdesign.com

Weird West Books
is an imprint of
Necro Publications
5139 Maxon Terrace
Sanford, FL 32771
necropublications.com

#2

THE
RED
SEVEN

ROBERT DEAN

For two women first:

Kay Bilotta and Julie Baier: Without your literary guid-
ance, where would I be? Without you and your love of
words, I'd be a different man. These notes, this music,
this rhythm is as much yours as it is mine.

And finally, for my wife:

Sarah Ann, you are my muse, my seductress - the most
beautiful girl in the world. You make a jazz horn swing.
I'm gonna prove your gamble on me was worth it.

"It's harder to heal than it is to kill."

      - Tamora Pierce

"There will be killing till the score is paid."

- Homer, *The Odyssey*

INTRODUCTION

One more crooked cross planted in the ground in the name of revenge. The dust settled, and the world was quiet. Birds sitting in the tall trees took a break from their throaty, melodious songs. The bugs buzzed less. The wind died off, holding its breath.

Off into the distance, a vulture sniffed death in the air. With great force, it took off toward the scent of demise.

When The Ghost fired the shot, the universe rode along with the spinning bullet. For a millisecond, all evil in the hearts of men ceased. The Ghost was righteous in this death because it was earned in the name of suffering.

Hidalgo would pay his debt to the devils below. For each death tallied under the heels of his boots, justice was served. The Ghost's pistol slipped out of his hands, and into the blood-stained grass.

Five of the men who soiled his family name lay in shallow graves. The others would get theirs just the same. Somewhere off in the distance, a crow squawked. No time to dwell in the moment. There was still much work to be done.

Hell still awaited The Ghost.

DANNY BOY

Horse hooves drifted across the muddy property. The sounds of the storm allowed cover onto the Masterson land. Seven men rode straight into infamy. Death stained their minds and destruction plagued their hearts. With each passing moment, the devil stalked closer to the home front.

A house sat on top of the hill while light flickered from the windows. Inside the home, the Masterson children helped mother set the table. Their father, Daniel, carved the bird. A fire popped and crackled, and smoke rose through the chimney and into the rainy night. This was a special evening. Mattie had news: she was in the family way. There'd be another Masterson running around soon.

Daniel slid his long, toothed knife along the meat of the turkey. The blade dove into the soft meat of the breast with ease. He felt proud about this moment; three pairs of eyes watched him with respect and admiration. He was daddy and the leader of the little Masterson clan. Like his father before him, he couldn't live without the love of these three heartbeats, each of them solely dependent on him.

When the glass from the window behind him shattered, a fear like no other surged through Daniel Masterson. Buckshot blasted through. Like trained soldiers, the Mastersons fell to

11

the floor. Daniel hollered to his brood, making sure no one was hit. There'd be hell to pay when he reached his gun.

Mattie and the children, Becky and Lucas, cowered in fear under the kitchen table. The draping arms of the tablecloth hid them from plain sight. The tears of the children stained Mattie's shirt, their cries reverberating into her bosom. The baby inside Mattie sensed the strife through the distress of his mother and thrashed inside her belly.

Daniel scrambled for his hunting rifle, and a chill crept into the house. With his gun raised, Daniel Masterson walked out of his front door and into oblivion.

Daniel knew within an instant his chances of surviving this night grew smaller with each drop of rain. Seven men sat on horses. Lightening flashed triumphant over mankind in the sky, the rider's eyes illuminated in the gloom as tunnels straight into hell.

The leader sat in the center, flanked by three desperados on each side. Seven road worn dogs with cold steel on their laps, shaped in a horseshoe of tragedy; seven riders on the fringes of death and depravity. Daniel Masterson looked at his eternity closing in upon him.

Daniel noticed the number seven with skull and crossbones on everything. Like the face of a playing card, the numeral featured on the riders' boots and sashes; it was even on their spurs.

The fabric of his shirt clung to his body, his hair pasted to his skull. His gun remained raised and aimed, despite changing his target with each small noise. Daniel waited for the next move.

"They call you the man-murderin' Ghost?" one called out. Thunder bowled in the distance. "The man they say cain't be seen in the night?" Another asked under the cover of the red bandanna covering his mouth.

"The cocksucker they say has cashed in more dead men than any bounty hunter alive?" Someone else called out while another whistled, mockingly.

Fear spiraled inside Daniel down to the pit of his stomach, and to the tips of his toes.

"That ain't me," Masterson replied. He swallowed hard and continued trying to escape the spider's nest. "Ain't no bounty hunters round here. I can promise you that. You got the wrong place. I ain't nothing but a simple man. A blacksmith. This here's my family land. I don't got nothin' to do with no slingin' guns." They wanted his brother. Daniel would do his best to protect him. Masterson's toes gripped the material inside of his boots. He waited for the reply of the inquisitor.

"Ain't the fuck I heard," the man said. "I heard The Ghost; the infamous man hunter stayed 'round these parts. Yep. Slept in a fine feather bed, on a few acres of mighty nice, green land. Say you're a blacksmith? This don't look like no simple blacksmith land, friend. Ain't no man on a blacksmith's wage gonna own land like this." His statement was correct; the Masterson family's plot was a sprawling piece of the American Dream. Their cabin was spacious and flocked by stunning oaks. The scene typically was picturesque. Even in the darkness, the space was open and inviting.

"Yessir. Blacksmithing's my trade. I'm a leather man, too. I ain't no bounty hunter. I don't have nothing to do with no outlaws. I keep to me and mine. I'd appreciate it if you fellers rode on. We got no business together." Masterson said, never lowering his weapon.

"A man hasta make a good livin' to have land. I bet it was paid with money from collecting the scalps of dead men."

The humor exited the rider's tone. "See here, we're looking for this Ghost feller. Don't go bullshittin' me you ain't heard of him. This Ghost here, he took the life of a business associate who owed money. We're here to collect on a debt owed." Someone cocked the hammer back on their pistol. The center horse stamped its feet, and steam rose from the great beast's nostrils.

Masterson paused for a dramatic moment. "There ain't no Ghost here. Only folks on this land are my kin and me. This don't look like no place where an outlaw lives. If there was, he'd be out here I reckon. I ain't him and he ain't here."

Inside the house, Mattie crept low. Mattie's heart rattled inside of its cage. She took a few breaths before daring to look outside. On her knees, her eyes peered over the window ledge. Seven men on horses surrounded her husband. His gun trembled; he was scared. Her right hand shook. The weight of the rusty pistol grew heavier with the passing seconds.

"Hear that boys? He ain't got nothin' to do with no bounty hunters. Sounds like we best take our sorry selves and go."

He paused, letting it hang like a dagger against the throat. "Sounds like buncha happy horseshit to me."

The rider in the middle blasted a shell into Daniel Masterson's left shoulder, near central mass.

Masterson's shotgun fired into the air. The blast stirred the horses, knocking the rider far to the right off his beast and face down in the mud. The fallen rider's fingers dug through the muck, trying to grab ahold of the sodden earth. His face was filthy with mud as he rose. Wiping his mouth clean, the rider sneered.

The rider's exposed face showed a scar leading from his nose to the right corner of the mouth.

Daniel aimed his rifle at the rider with the scar, intending to blow his brains out. A shot came from one of the other's Colt .45, the bullet hitting the barrel of Daniel's shotgun, sending it flying out of his hands.

The six riders cackled. The man with the scar wanted blood. He had a name: Cortez. The rains continued in a terrible fury.

"Get up, motherfucker," Cortez hissed.

Daniel looked into the eyes of a predator. History was intertwined with the damned, and he was destined to dance.

The pain in Daniel's shoulder ached, but his foe was injured, too. He must have broken his collarbone in the fall. At least they were both handicapped.

Daniel took a long swing, landing a punch to Cortez's jaw. The rest of the riders hollered and cheered. Shaking it off, Cortez squared away and charged forward, delivering two hooks to Daniel's midsection. The wind blew out of his belly as he sagged forward. Nearly landing a knockout blow, Cortez lost his footing and leaned forward an inch too far, giving Daniel the edge to land a knuckled devastator to Cortez's right cheek.

Answering the attack, Cortez flung his muddy boot into Daniel's leg, sending him down a few inches, and with the dirty move, Cortez grabbed a hold of Daniel, biting his ear. Daniel screamed. Blood filled Cortez's mouth. The men on their horses laughed like they'd never seen something so funny. Daniel's left elbow connected to Cortez's stomach, sending each of them back into the filth of the wet ground below.

A single blast fired from the window. Mattie howled, witness to the love of her life struggling with who she knew was his killer. Five of the riders dismounted, walking past the battle at their feet. They laughed and whistled, and headed for the house. Some of them began to undo their bandannas while the big one took out his buck knife.

The center rider hopped off his horse and watched the fight continue. Daniel Masterson became a wild animal. An unrelenting rage surged through him. Mattie's screams electrified his blood. The vision of his children being harmed broke the human element inside. Through the pain in his shoulder, he dove for Cortez, bringing him to the earth once again. Trying his hardest to kill the man, Daniel Masterson's arms landed a few punches as the boggy ground enveloped them. Cortez swung hard from under Daniel and landed a cross blow to the jaw.

Frightened yelps rose through the thunder as Mattie and the children faced five foul beasts, draped in depravity. Beyond the hills, the roaming wolves howled at the rain-soaked moon.

"My brother don't live here!" Daniel hollered. The other rider who didn't go inside stood in the downpour, statuesque. He remained silent. Cortez and Daniel Masterson got to their feet and exchanged pitiless blows.

"We're simple folk! Please, we didn't do anything to no one! I ain't him." Masterson screamed. Daniel landed a haymaker to Cortez.

Dazed, Cortez slumped forward. The silent man came forward, swung from the back and connected his fist to Daniel Masterson's face. Blackness.

A familiar, toxic taste splashed across Daniel's lips, bringing him back to life. His eyes opened through the layers of grime and blood. He was covered in kerosene. The two men stood over him, throwing liquid in fantastic, pernicious waves.

Daniel Masterson found his footing to challenge the two men, but as he was in the crawling ape stance, Hidalgo blew a fist-sized hole into his belly.

The world went into a frantic, God-awful zenith of terror and pain. The kerosene spilled into his two wounds, robbing his body of sanity.

"The Ghost's yer fuckin' brother? Well, I reckon this is gonna make him mighty upset. Cause cousin, meet my brother!" Cortez said. He towered over Daniel, his shirt wrapped inside his fist, about to deliver a final blow. The front door to the house was wide open while screams of horror emanated into the night air. Even in the rain, and through his haze, Daniel's heart broke. He'd failed his family.

"Yer brother is gonna be one mad son of a bitch." He spit into the brown ocean that surrounded them. "I want him to know it was me. I want him to know it was The Red Seven gang that ruined his life. He ain't bigger than death."

Cortez let the body of Daniel Masterson fall back into the gloam.

Hidalgo remained silent. His brother looked at him, almost bored, and nodded. Hidalgo took one last puff off his cigarillo and dropped it into the puddle of kerosene. The flames rose into torrid waves of blue and orange. Hidalgo made the sign of the cross. Cortez fired his pistol into the fire. Daniel Masterson was dead.

The thunder echoed deep in the canyons and valleys. Cortez and Hidalgo walked toward the house. Filthy hands and hungry mouths, tired after a long ride, would devour the feast of turkey with the trimmings. The tatters of Mattie's dress lay on the ground.

The Red Seven slept in the beds of the family they murdered, and not a one of them had nightmares. They slept in salacious, perfect peace.

《《 — 》》

The Ghost watched the townspeople of Madrid, Texas ebb and flow as they carried out their daily errands. Mothers dragged sons along as desperados on horses clicked through town.

The Ghost sat in the shadows of the porch of the Landmark Hotel.

The rays of the Texas sun pummeled everything it touched. Sweat dripped off the tips of his mustache. It was a morbid heat. He took a long pull from his beer mug and waited.

A long time passed after the murders. For over a year, he laid low, wrapping his head around the horror of losing his family. Usually, The Ghost was stoic, unshakeable, but for a period, the world sickened him. His brother's little family rested beyond the pond, toward the pines where his mother and father laid. The makeshift cemetery was the most important spot in the world to him. His flesh and blood invested their souls into that soil; it was sacred ground.

Winslow S. Elliot, the Masterson's closest friend, lived a few miles away from the pastoral, family property. He was unlucky enough to stumble upon the carnage out in the flowery acres of the Masterson land.

When The Ghost returned from a long sojourn out on the trails, he returned to a home that was not the one he'd left long ago. It was desolate and cold. It had been empty for some time. Alarmed, The Ghost rode to see Elliot to hear the tale. When he sat at his old friend's table, he looked into the eyes of a man who had a terrible story to tell.

The Ghost and Elliot sat in a tormented silence over cups of black coffee. They drank in the spectacular sights of the Elliot land. Wildflowers bloomed. Mexican hats, Alamo fires, and bluebonnets dotted the landscape. Ash and Cedar hugged the natural cone of the earth where the cabin was cradled.

The dozen or so head of cattle roamed free and chewed on the lush grass.

The wild world stopped for no man, and no tragedy. The Ghost and Elliot took in the moment and accepted their meeting for all of its terrible flaws, for what it was: an exorcism of the phantoms of the past. Closure for the damned, but persecution for the guilty soul; The Ghost let the universe take the reigns.

Elliot slid The Ghost the note left by The Red Seven across the table.

Dear 'Spook,

You can thank yerself for yer brother resting in his pine box. Shouldn'ta takin whut weren't yers—law or no law.

Don't bother tryin' to hunt us, bounty hunter. The Red Seven gang is no moar. Shouldn'ta collected that head down in New Orleans. Yer brother'd be livin' otherwise.

See you in hell. Give yer brother our warmist.

"I was supposed to see Daniel not but two days later. I'd ast him to put shoes on one my hosses, said he'd help me out. When I got up there, boy, I about keeled over." The old man said with a profound, deep sadness in his voice. He'd known Daniel since he was a child. When the Masterson parents slid into their graves, Winslow Elliot became the sage guardian of the family; he'd even walked Mattie down the aisle.

Seeing their bodies laying in the twisted mess tore up his soul. Speaking to The Ghost, he fought back the tears. Devastation danced across the lines in his face.

"I'll spare you the finer details, leave it at it weren't pretty," Elliot said, reliving the terrible scene. The steam rose off his coffee and danced into the air. The Ghost absorbed the words, processed them and took a moment before answering the old man.

"I wanna hear it. Don't spare my feelings. What's done is done."

Winslow looked out into the wild expanse of his acreage. The tall grasses swayed in a dramatic wave under the arms of the oak trees. The orchestra of birds off in the distance calmed his heart. The coffee tasted like blood. Anything tasted sour to Elliot when he relived that day. For months, he doubted there was anything good left in the world.

"Fine, then I ain't gonna sugarcoat it," Elliot said with finality.

"Much obliged."

Elliot looked down into the black broth inside his cup. He kept his head toward the table, refusing to look The Ghost in the eyes for this part of the story.

"They burnt him up. Like a trash heap, they lit Daniel on fire. I ain't ever seen a man burned up before, and I'll tell ye it scared the bejesus outta me. I found what was left of the man I seent grow up from a lad; couldn't even recognize him. A Goddamned charred black boned mess. Looked like he crawled out of the pits of Satan's hell, he was Goddamned ghastly. Broke my heart, it did. I cried for a good few minutes before I dared go in that house. You see a man in a burned heap, you ain't no fool knowin' the house weren't gonna be pretty. After I had collected myself, I pulled my blaster off the hoss. The old man slid his fingers through his wavy mane.

"Wasn't takin' no chances. I gathered my guts and hollered for Mattie, hoping her n' the kids was ok. I turned the corner into the house, and my God. Was hell on earth. A Goddamn bloodbath in there. They put a bullet into the boy straight away. He was hiding under a table, and one-a those sons of bitches musta seent him cause, one shot did the trick. That little body covered in blood. I never in all my goddamned days seent something so horrific. " The old man trailed off for a moment. His voice broke with emotion.

Explaining what he saw drudged up some deep-seated feelings. He took a long breath and continued. "As for Mattie and Becky, well, they had their way with each of them poor girls. When they was done, each of the girls took a bullet to the head."

"What about the seven on the door?" The Ghost asked.

"Well, Mattie, God rest her soul, was nearby the door. She was in bad shape. They used a knife before they put a bullet in her head."

The old man paused. He took a drink. The Ghost was off where cognitive thought and the abstract ability to piece together tragedy lie beyond the horizon. A dull, heart-crushing rage brewed inside.

"They ransacked the place. We did our best at trying to put it together so yew wouldn't have to see it like we did. It broke my spirit cleaning that blood. No matter how hard I tried, that blood won't come outta that door. I'm right sorry you saw it. I been dreading this day."

The Ghost looked awful. "They left this note for ye, and that seven on the door. Who'd do such a thing? Who'd ye cross? You had to make a man hate your goddamned guts for this to happen, son." For a few seconds, the silence between the two men was dense, like a culpable fog of assumption. The Ghost felt poisoned with guilt. It hung at the back of his throat, acidic.

The Ghost spoke. "Was down in New Orleans when I sniffed out a real son of bitch. This piece of work would rob his own mother blind for few bucks to spend in a whorehouse. He'd murder a child for a few sips of rotgut."

"Big money?" Elliot asked.

"Real big money. Wanted all over the California territory for grand larceny, and killed a few in the interior. Someone out in Tennessee wanted him dead. Bad. Bad enough that they put a heavy price on the cocksucker's tombstone. Name was Sampson Elbridge, a real ugly fucker. Had big bucked teeth and lips looked like he ate a hornet's nest. Somehow this here boy landed in New Orleans. He lied his way onto a dock, unloading ships when he wasn't stealing off 'em."

"People'll do anything to make a Goddamned dollar."

"Went by David Stockdale. He'd set himself up real good. The perfect crime almost: had a whole setup going. Steal a few boxes and send em down toward the Chalmette battlefield where a feller'd unload the goods, and they'd store everything for sale on the black market. For every twenty crates of goods, one might disappear, twenty-four hours a day. Their little boat ran down the river at all hours of the night. Pretty ingenious. He was the boss, who was gonna complain? The shipping clerks acted none the wiser. Stores got less product than ordered, but the whole crew on the dock got a cut of the action. Keep their traps shut and wham, easy money."

The Ghost pulled a cigarillo to his lips. With a wooden match, he created the spark.

"How'd ye come to hear about him?" Elliot asked.

"When folks get comfortable—they get sloppy. Our man Mr. Stockdale, or Elbridge, got cocky and started running his mouth off. If you're running an illegal operation and slapping around some lowlifes, what makes you think they aren't gonna squeal for a few bones themselves? I reckon one of em saw his face on a Wanted poster, and that's all she wrote."

"People get to talking."

"Always do. Fore' I know it, I hear about a bounty down in New Orleans when I was in Alabama cleaning up the mess some scalp hunters made. I hear about an easy take, so I rode down. It wasn't no trouble at all sniffing him out." The Ghost relaxed for a few milliseconds, but soon enough his heart hurt again.

"Go on, I wanna hear how this whole mess started," Elliot said.

"I bought some clothes off an old deckhand and blended into the faces of the crowd. I see one of the guys and ask if they'd put me on for the day. I spun a pretty good yarn and next thing I know I'm moving crates for a day's wage. I'm watching everything and everyone. His network was in full swing. While Elbridge marked off the legit goods coming in, his boys found stuff worth selling and slipped a few of each off and on the private boat. He kept two logs of what was moving and where. I was impressed by how smooth he ran these two crews without much fuss.

"Elbridge made a comment about me being on the level. He wanted to tell me the rules of their game pretty quick. A new deckhand wasn't about to mess up their routine. I played dumb.

"I paid mind to his actions, how he worked a straight job like a criminal. He didn't try to hide who he was; to him, it was one big joke. 'Stockdale.'"

"I hate men like that. If you're gonna be a crook, at least, be a humble one," Elliot said.

"Right quick I knew I had my man. My leads told me to pay attention to the lisp from getting kicked in the face by an Appaloosa as a child. This man sure as hell had a lisp and didn't sound like he was a Creole. I heard him tell stories about his past life. Didn't hide a thing. The son of a bitch was brazen. He dared someone to come collect the bounty far as I'm concerned."

The clouds in the sky moved into one another, drifting from shapes of children's toys into sweet serenity. Elliot's property was a far cry from the chaos of New Orleans. The Ghost continued.

"The steamboats honked and hollered. I drifted up behind him and announced his Christian name—Elbridge, not Stockdale. When he spun around on his heels, ready to either fight or shoot, I took the top of his head off."

"Didn't give him a chance to go alive?"

"Why bother? I'd rather just kill 'em."

"Fair enough."

"Turns out the money he funneled from those stolen goods went into a kitty to pay off the debt to our friends The Red Seven. Got caught up in the opium trade with some Chinamen, and next thing he knew his balls were in a sling. Couldn't keep his hands off the goods. The Red Seven wanted his money, and his head."

He was already haunted; a man with demons for days. Now this. The Ghost ran his fingers over the cold steel of his revolver. Elliot said nothing.

"When The Red Seven came to see Daniel, it was me they wanted. I'm the reason my brother is dead. All because I killed a cheap, two-bit hustler. He owed them money. And you can't collect on the dead without hurting the living." His words sunk like daggers.

Elliot slammed his fist down on the wooden table. Rings reverberated through the coffee in his cup, creating small waves.

"Those men are dogs. If it wern't yer brother, it'd been one else's. Can't take the past back. They'd kill anyone in their way, that's goddamned clear as the nose on your face, son. I don't think your friend Elbridge was reason, he was an excuse. The one thing you can do is to ride on with his memory in yer heart, young feller. Those men stole anything worth a cent, all you did was give 'em justification to their crime. Seeing Daniel's body broke my heart. I love you just as I loved him. But, don't blame yerself. Hell, they even stole yer brother's lucky brand."

«« — »»

Upon his return home, The Ghost intended to take a break. He'd been out there too long and had seen too much. The reality of a brutal world sunk their claws into him any chance they could. His soul was tired.

The plan was to lie low, get reacquainted with family life again, and to have a relationship with his kin beyond letters or the occasional visit. While those knew him as The Ghost out there, in the living world, he was just as ethereal at home. His niece and nephew knew him more from stories than actual time spent.

After the last marathon of a bounty, he deserved quiet mornings and fire in the hearth, not out in the elements. For six months The Ghost chased a man named Colm Beattie, a known child killer and dog fighter who'd escaped every set of shackles ever placed on his wrists. Many folks swore he was the Devil's personal missionary of pain. Whatever two-bit town Beattie slid into, suffering followed.

Despite being wanted across the upper reaches of No Man's Land out where Oklahoma met Texas, no one had come close to cashing in on Beattie's head. The man was resourceful. The Ghost met with bereaved mothers and fathers with hate deep in their hearts. Men wept as they told the tale of burying their children. The longer he worked Beattie's trail of lies, the deeper he fell into the madness that surrounded Beattie or John Anderson, or Cam Beatle or whatever assumed name he'd go by when establishing himself in a new town. And as always, the narrative was the same: Beattie would get the lay of the land, and soon, kids would come up missing.

The Ghost traveled a lot of miles and saw Beattie's handiwork; it was a crisscross of terror that gripped communities across the plains. Children slashed to ribbons with a long skinning knife.

The people's misery was heartbreaking, but what tore a hole in The Ghost's soul was stumbling into Beattie's mother's house in Texarkana.

A white shack down a long road and off behind a gaggle of trees and overgrown bushes, if you didn't know what you were searching for, you'd never see it. When The Ghost broke through the boarded up door, he entered a cavern of hell he'd never imagined.

The den of a child killer was gruesome enough, but Beattie took trophies. The macabre collection was vast and on display. A sickness hung in the air. As The Ghost walked through the dusty museum of death with both guns drawn, he felt like the stories were true: Colm Beattie was, in fact, a part of hell's army.

When he saw the skulls sitting on the kitchen counter, he knew this was not a man of this world, but a madman set out to punish mankind.

Seeing the rusty knives and the blood dried on children's clothes snapped something inside of The Ghost. Every few feet something insidious lay on the ground with bloodstains. The buckboard house had light streaming through in certain spots from Mother Nature's wear and tear.

The Ghost was used to the average gunslinger with a head full of opium and a score to settle, not this. This room, these artifacts of finality tattooed themselves on his heart and late at night he'd never forget seeing inside of the mind of a man who murdered little bodies with tiny hands and dirty faces.

When The Ghost finally caught up with Colm Beattie, he was posing as a butcher in Batesville, Arkansas. In the past half a year, he'd learned so much about Beattie, he didn't need to ask questions and he didn't need a description or to double-check his work. When he saw his man, The Ghost got within a breath and pulled the trigger in the child killer's face till his gun went click.

The locals dragged Beattie's body out into the streets. The famed murderer was put on display as the local photographer snapped a few brown photos for the history books. Children slapped the dead body while some of the adults took anything of value off his corpse.

The Ghost felt like he'd poured everything out of himself after that job. He needed a long rest. Coming over the hill and landing back into the Masterson universe, he expected tranquility. What he got instead shattered his broken heart.

For over a year, The Ghost lived in the empty, quiet house. He kept to himself, trying to recoup his sanity, his sense of being. He took long looks at the empty bedrooms. What remained of Daniel's things he took care of like they were priceless. For a while, just being there was comforting, but like all things in The Ghost's world, the debt owed needed to be paid in full.

《《 — 》》

The Ghost watched his father's home burn to the ground. The house he and his brother were born and raised in. The dipper shined bright while the rest of the stars twinkled in accepted retribution. His father would understand. Winslow Elliot helped their father construct the house; their sweat was in the fibers of the building.

Just the same, he'd never want his surviving son to live with the brutal reminder of his awful loss. The fire slinked up the front door, and as the bloodstained wood bathed in flame, the mordant seven burned.

The tall grasses swayed like the waves of the ocean on a rocky voyage, and the world stopped at your feet when sitting out on the porch, watching the sun dip off into the west. A small stream crossed the edge of the property where the deer drank. The Masterson land signified what manifest destiny was anchored in.

He stood in silence, watching the fire eat his memories. The coyotes off in the distance howled behind the hills.

When it was all over he'd return and build a majestic new house, taller and bigger, a tribute to the loss. Till then, the land was in the care of Winslow S. Elliot. A garden would grow in his mother's name.

«« — »»

The Ghost landed in Memphis on the back of his horse, Chalky, following a string of cold leads. He'd been searching for anything, something. He'd been out aimlessly following leads for over a year now, making it two years since the murder of his family. After crawling out of a dark depression following Daniel's death, his resolve was simple: kill them all.

When he finally shook out the cobwebs inside, the time had passed.

All the tricks of the trade he worked in his bounty hunter days weren't adding up to the capture of The Red Seven. Despite the gang having a large federal bounty on their heads, none of the other bounty hunters cashed them in. They vanished into thin air and without a bang on Main Street, USA. Sometimes bad men go out robbing a bank as a final middle finger in the air—The Red Seven dissolved into the unearthly realm and did a damn fine job of covering their tracks.

Their slip into the civilian world was a good one. But, like all humans, criminals make mistakes. It was a matter of ferreting out the scent. Humans are creatures of habit, and when one domino falls, the rest follow.

There was a considerable price tag on their heads. A cool hundred each was the asking price for Hiladgo and Cortez, the bosses. The remaining five were at fifty apiece.

This wasn't about the money; it was a reckoning. Bonded by the ink of a dead America, he'd light the dollar bills on fire. Murder for hire or solicited revenge, it depended on which way a man viewed the glass.

Judge G. Nazarko from Texas signed off on the blood of The Red Seven. The grace of the American people's safety was the guise of the signature.

Rob enough banks and trains, people want your head; blow away a few people standing in line just for kicks? They want your head on a silver platter. Under the current tally, The Red Seven were held accountable for at least twenty killings, and more stolen money than a small bank held. They'd stolen ponies and broken every law held dear by the emerging America. Posses and lawmen alike came up short or on the wrong end of a gun when dealing with the most famous gang in the west. By all estimates, The Red Seven's business was good. The judge was happy to sign their scalps away.

Following a small outlaw trail, he wound up in Memphis. The Ghost took up in a bare-bones room in a roach motel. He drifted in and out of the local shitholes, mixing it up with the toothless vagrants cadging for a drink. He asked around: who knew what, etc. He made acquaintances with a few of the townie scumbags.

He roamed the streets, hanging with the hustlers, sitting in sketchy trenches. Nothing came up. Another town searched, and another disappointment. Memphis was a bust. It was late, and he'd decided to ride out. He was headed toward Little Rock because he'd heard murmurs. Like Memphis and the rest the towns, it was a shot in the dark. This was a chess match, every move counted.

He'd stabled Chalky at a small spot off the edge of town. The joint was a ramshackle affair, cheap, but the horses were well cared for. It was in the saddle room where The Ghost saw the symbol: his brother's shamrock.

Burned into a saddle, and sitting next to his on the high wooden shelves. He ran his fingers across the grooves in the burned leather. The saddle was new. An aching sadness engulfed him, feeling the curves of the cloverleaves, and he felt alone in the world. Four leaves, and four of his family dead; his stomach sank. Whoever owned this saddle was about to see the image of a man possessed.

The Ghost limped over to the little old Mexican running the joint, asking a litany of questions, his face flush and ashen. He needed to know who owned this saddle. He'd paint the doors of the barn red in blood if it were one of the men on the wanted poster he kept close to his heart.

The Ghost paced in the darkness of the barn. The ember of his cigarillo acted as a beacon in the gloom. Chalky stomped his feet and put his head close to The Ghost's chest as he patted his long skull.

31

Riders came and went; no one touched the shamrock saddle. The old man watched The Ghost, trying to understand why a saddle was so important.

It was in his best interest to let the man dressed in black do whatever he needed to. The Ghost promised he'd pay double if there were a mess to clean up.

The sun would rise soon. The dampness in the air signaled the coming of a new day. A raven-haired cowboy appeared. Drunk, he stumbled into the saddle room and pulled out the shamrock saddle. The Ghost sized the drunk up as he laid his saddle blanket down over a molasses-colored pinto. The drunk was sluggish and staggering; he'd hit the bottle all night long. He'd fall asleep on top of his horse.

The drunk slipped his boot into the stirrups, and just as he was about to throw the other foot over the back of the beast, stars danced across his eyes. The Ghost swung hard behind the drunk and connected his fist to the base of the skull.

The drunk's foot fell out of the stirrup; he took the fall face first, twisting his ankle sideways. The drunk crumpled in the hay covering the ground. The side of his temple shined wet with crimson.

The Ghost cocked his pistol and then rammed it into the gaping mouth of the frightened drunk. The man's trousers became dark with urine. His hands sprung up, and his cries were muffled as the gun scraped his windpipe.

"I'm gonna to ask you once. You lie, I'll know. Want your brains splattered all over this filthy floor? Where'd you get this saddle?" The Ghost demanded.

The drunk choked from the gun in his throat, unable to provide an answer aside from rhythmic gags. The Ghost leaned in harder, before pulling the barrel of the gun out of the man's mouth. A long strand of spit hung off the iron.

The Ghost rapped the gun across the man's lips. Blood splotches erupted to the epidermal center.

"Tell me why this shamrock is on your saddle or I'm pulling this trigger against the side of your fuckin' head."

The man stared down the barrel of the revolver. The Ghost's fist smashed the seeping wound on the side of the man's head to jog his memory.

"Take it! Take the Goddamned saddle!"

"Don't want it. I wanna know where *you* got it." The Ghost raised his arm up again, ready to strike. This next blow may not be so kind to leave the drunkard conscious.

"Feller over in Texas! I was runnin' cattle as a pickup job, and he custom makes saddles. I ain't nothing but a cowboy. Ain't got no family, just a treat for my hard work! Honest, take it!" His breath stunk of cheap hooch.

"Texas is a big place. Best start getting real specific." The Ghost dropped to his knees, right on the man's arms, crushing them.

The old Mexican who owned the place stood at his porch watching, but hidden. He hoped he didn't have to clean up another body. The Ghost placed the barrel of the pistol between the man's eyes. The steel was cold. The Ghost cocked the trigger and the man spoke:

"Tiny place, south of Austin, makes the saddles. Do leather work. Call him Danny Boy cause he's a Mick." The Ghost's knees pressed deeper into the flesh, causing an awful pain, tearing the muscle.

"Madrid! Madrid, Texas! I swear to it!"

He stood up and un-cocked his pistol. The little boozehound wasn't lying. There was nothing to lose. While he was a punk, he was too stupid, small and weak to ever ride with one under the color red. No one would employ a bum like him on a significant score. He was small peanuts.

The Ghost mounted Chalky and took off. The man lay there crying and thankful to be alive. When the drunk managed to get to his feet, he pulled a long slug out of the bottle in his satchel with shaky hands.

The Ghost rode southwest, down into Arkansas through the night. His sweat-drenched legs ached, and he'd woke up in his saddle more than once. With each mile underfoot, he punished his horse. Mid-afternoon he couldn't ride a mile farther. Chalky shook, exhausted from the long journey deep into the galloping hills of the Arkansas country. All around, choirs of birds sang, and the wind tickled the tall wild grass. The land was beautiful and striking. It looked as good a place as any for a nap. He set up his bedroll under a swath of long-armed live oaks.

The fantasy of seeing his wish for retribution come true danced in his head as his eyes shuttled off into dreamland. The brutality of men, the central arc to the history books and the King James Bible. Men kill without reason, and men kill because they feel powerful sitting atop a throne of skulls. A crippling darkness lurks within the hearts of the entire human animal; it was a part of the agreement with God; free will is a compromise to be made to rise above the apes. A man's desire to destroy is quelled by his good sense or sense of righteousness.

The Ghost knew both sides of the coin. He'd cut so many men down over the years.

He watched scores die in the war and watched the survivors fight a silent battle in the real world. The slow expanse of the wilderness crept around him and his sleeping horse. They slept into the early evening.

He'd made it to a small town along the Texas/Arkansas border. He sent a telegram to an informant down in Austin. What the drunk said was true: there was a leatherman out in Madrid who went by the name of Danny Boy McKay.

He craved catharsis and closure. Wounds of the damned never close easy. Hiding for the night in the arms of a nightmare was the way he knew how to survive such a cruel, cold world. Hell was at his heels and the winds of reckoning to his back.

He rose before dawn and rode out like a man possessed. The low hills and lush malachite valleys passed mile after mile; his eyes never left the road ahead. He swore he'd let the horse relax if he rode hard and true for his rider these last grueling miles.

«« — »»

Madrid was nothing special. The hand-painted signs were faded and used, a layer of filth covered what the eye saw. What was once white looked gray. Anything once straight hung with a deranged sense of sadness, even the dirt felt of a lower order. The local whores sat annoyed, struggling with the weight of the world on one hand, and the dim prospects to make a buck on the other.

From the looks of his hotel, it had seen some action. The Ghost let the world move around him while he waited till the time was right. Second by second, the anticipation of the day wore heavy on The Ghost's soul. But, this had to be done right, and without any bullshit.

Waiting was the hardest part of this job. Minutes took eons. The spinning wheels of a ghastly world moved into machinations for predatory deliverance. He was ready. The Ghost sipped his beer. The long, straight brim of his hat sat low over his eyes.

From head to toe, The Ghost wore black, the color of a preacher. Being a man who presents men to their maker, it was only right to carry the color of collapse. He was a man trapped in the puzzle of mourning.

The hotel's piano player toiled away at the keys, trying his hardest to bang out a recognizable song through the miserable day drunk he incurred. Veins of malicious sweat flowed like small rivers down his neck and face; his concentration was to keep upright, and alive. He tried to be there as a fixture instead of traipsing through the song, whatever it might have been. The detailed flourishes of a master's hand were omnipresent at plenty of hotels around the world, just not today and not here.

Last night's whiskey talked, and the drunken piano player's fingers followed. His song was ugly and wrong. Finally, he found a pocket and rode it out. It was a jangled, whiskey-soaked rendition of *The Camptown Lady*.

The Ghost ignored the hackneyed musical abortion in the parlor. His blood surged while he let the anticipation of death percolate under the blackness.

Before The Ghost left his room, he equipped himself. The ritual. Always the same, a checks and balances system of inventory:

- Small snub-nose .22-caliber pistol up the right sleeve of his jacket
- Two revolvers: One on his side and one above belt buckle
- Boot knife
- Papers stating he was a law certified bounty hunter under Federal Law
- Gun at each side, and sometimes one against his belt buckle

When he put a bullet in Danny Boy's skull, the signature of the Honorable Judge G. Nazarko would liberate him from any bullshit the local sheriff may present depending on Danny Boy's status these years as a typical citizen.

The clock struck noon. The Ghost got up and left an almost full beer for a rummy to cop a cheap buzz.

He strolled toward Danny Boy's massive wooden shed at the edge of town. The hot, red clay clung to the toes of his boots.

Overhead, a few crows sat on the spire of the local church, watching the man in black walk toward retribution. They cawed and squawked, giving Danny Boy a sign the angel of death was a foot from his door. The Irishman never heard their calls. He was too busy working the hide over a custom saddle for the local undertaker. Oh, sweet irony.

The Ghost reached the site. A sickening sense of disgust washed over as he stood under the smuggest reminder of carelessness a man could post: above the front door to the workshop was his brothers Shamrock, only forty times the size. It was painted green, joking to come on inside and bring the kids.

Daniel Masterson's soul and shamrock weren't Danny Boy's to mock. His fatal mistake was his brazen, self-satisfied ego. Danny Boy paraded his past in sadistic symbols, and he'd die for it.

The smell inside the shop was pungent, the air pregnant with toxicity, heavy salt and old flesh.

An old timer sat at a table with his leather knife, surrounded by piles of rawhide. The geezer's gnarled hands worked a piece of leather over and over; the ancient bastard was precise. Each of the old man's movements meant something.

The Ghost approached, and the old man looked him over, above the lens of his glasses. He took a moment to study The Ghost before addressing him.

A haunting sensation crept over the geezer. Gloom surrounded this stranger; a man of his demeanor didn't roll into his shop. The old man set his leather knife down.

"Help ye, son?" The geezer asked.

"Not unless you're Danny Boy McKay."

The old man looked him over for a beat before speaking.

"You got anger in them eyes, boy."

"Unsatisfied customer." The Ghost replied, almost with a smirk.

"I can see ye ain't comin' round here fer hugs and kisses. And no sir, I ain't Danny." The Ghost observed the scars littering the old man's hands from decades of abuse. The old man's knuckles were huge. The crisscross of white slashes and scars made anyone wonder how such a mangled pair of paws, could work so perfectly amidst the meaty chaos.

"I ain't your boy. We ain't friendly. Where's Danny?" The Ghost moved in a foot closer. The old man felt the anger swelling.

"Calm down there. Didn't mean nothin' by it. He ain't round." The geezer fibbed. This wasn't his first rodeo.

The Ghost took a step closer. The heels of his boots sounded brash and cumbersome in the room. A terse second of silence passed between, like a dance of Mexican gunfighters.

The old man took note of the gun at The Ghost's belt, and the one at his side. He knew a gunslinger when he saw one.

"I've seent a man with a score to settle plenty of times at my age, and you ain't a nun seeking pennies for heaven."

The Ghost pulled out his revolver. He didn't aim it but held it in his right hand. His thumb rubbed over the hammer.

"Danny Boy. We ain't got no business together."

The old man eyed the black-cloaked desperado. His old bones stood up and moved over toward The Ghost. His feet dragged along the dusty wooden floor. Standing six feet apart, he saw the seriousness carved in the broad lines of The Ghost's weathered face. The old man wasn't stupid. Danny was there. He knew Danny's past and did his best diverting any of the past transgressions befallen the young McKay.

"I tell you feller, Danny ain't here, and we don't want any trouble."

"Ain't here for trouble."

A moment passed between them. The Ghost recognized the situation for what it was—this old man was protecting Danny Boy.

Danny appeared from the back and onto the scene. He carried a large skinning knife and wore a stained tanning apron. He wasn't the gunslinger The Ghost expected, but a round-faced simpleton.

His beady eyes spaced far apart, he took labored breaths with his mouth instead of his nose. The Ghost couldn't believe this creature was a part of The Red Seven. He looked like an overgrown child.

Danny Boy paused, aware something hung diseased in the air. For a few seconds, no one spoke. Danny Boy was smaller than The Ghost expected. Even though Danny Boy had an outlaw past, he exuded lap dog, not a serial killer.

"S'wrong, paw?" Danny Boy inquired.

Danny Boy knew the man in black was no friend.

"Son, this man here says you has business together." The old man said. The disappointment was apparent in his voice from his son's entrance at the exact wrong moment.

"You sneaky old son of a bitch," The Ghost hissed. He fixed his attention to Danny Boy, who by now tried inching to a better position for coverage. He froze as The Ghost's eyes fell on him. Danny Boy wasn't as stupid as he looked.

"Recognize me, Danny?"

"No, sir, I don't. I don't know who you are."

"Come on. Use your imagination."

"Can't say I reckon I know who you are," Danny said. He was nervous. His voice shook. The Ghost raised his widowmaker toward Danny Boy's face. Danny's voice jumped a few octaves.

"Sir, I got no idea who you are. We crossed paths?" Danny asked, wishing he could move fast enough to gut this man, or bash his head in. He knew better than to go first. He knew exactly who he was at first sight.

"Danny, you're just being cute. I know you're putting on a show for your paw." He took a beat. "Danny Boy, you've had nightmares about me." The Ghost's eyes looked extra dark as the brim of his hat shaded them, giving him an unearthly appearance.

"The hell's he talking bout, boy?" the old man demanded. He darted looks between his son and the man who never broke his stare at the doomed.

Danny's brain scrambled trying to surmise the next movement. He might land the knife if he could get a few steps closer. He couldn't be lazy because he knew the stories. The Ghost's speed with his pistol was barroom legend. Danny Boy was the walking dead.

The Ghost kept his aim on him. Off in the distance of the town's limits, booming church bells rang, signaling the hour. The sun turned its broiler up a few clicks, cooking anyone in its gaze.

"You may think your boy here ran with the wrong crowd. May have stolen horses, or maybe even got into a gunfight once or twice. Nothing a small stint in the clink couldn't cure. Danny here, well he's wanted clear across the country. Your boy here is a killer."

The old man said nothing. The color drained from his face. The Ghost continued, realizing the sense of theater.

"Yessir. Danny Boy's killed a lot of people. Stolen plenty of money from the banks. Bet you didn't know he was an outlaw, did you?"

"Paw—he's lyin' I swear." Danny Boy tried to cut in.

"You shut the fuck up. Grown folks are talking," The Ghost answered him cold. Danny Boy stood dumb-faced and tragic while The Ghost laid it out.

"This is news to me." The old man sighed.

"Reason I'm here 'fore you today is this piece of shit murdered my family. Raped my niece, raped my brother's wife. They're both dead. Put a bullet in my nephew, right in his head. My fucking brother was lit on fire."

The Ghost spat at Danny Boy's feet. The father's mouth hung open; shocked he sired such a monster. The blood flowed like molten lava, The Ghost's eyes yellowed with contempt.

"That's why I'm here." He continued with his story, daring Danny Boy to make a move as he spilled the guts of the story.

"And that fucking shamrock you mark on all of your saddles? It was my brother's. I know because I helped forge it."

Danny searched his father's disgusted face.

The brand sat in the fire, the flames kissing the iron; it burned orange and molten, ready for pressing.

"Ye rotten, no good bastard. I knew yew was wrong. If this man is telling the truth, yer low. Ye killed a woman and her babies? I'm ashamed." The old man looked hurt.

Danny Boy said nothing. Shame overtook him. For a millisecond, he looked down at the leather-carving blade in his right hand. He considered his options.

He'd have to do something and fast if there was any shot out of feigning a defense.

Acting in cowardice, Danny Boy thrust his father into The Ghost. The old man sailed like a sack of pebbles. Despite Danny's stupid exterior, he was all thug muscle. Planning wasn't his strong suit, throwing his weight around was. The old man knocked them both to the floor.

The old man's knife sunk into The Ghost's shoulder. The blade's extreme serrations and rough edge tore through the muscle.

Pulling the blade out, The Ghost threw the bloody knife to the ground. He fired his revolver at Danny Boy's head. Danny dove behind the desk. Distress plunged plausible scenarios from Danny Boy's head. Any movement he made wasn't invested in anything except panic. Firing the pistol The Ghost guessed was in the drawer, Danny Boy missed all six shots in a quick succession. Dread led his bullets askew.

The Ghost landed a shot square in his central mass. Blood splattered the table. Danny screamed. The second shot hit his left hand, shattering the bone into fragments, and knocking the pistol to the floor. His shots were sharp.

The old man lay in a ball on the filthy workshop floor.

"Please don't murder my son." The old man wheezed as he looked at the rising Ghost. Tears streamed down his face.

"Might wanna close your eyes," The Bounty Hunter answered.

His hat lay on the dirty floor. Slipping it back over his head, he took deliberate steps.

Standing over the criminal, The Ghost shot Danny Boy once more in his left knee. The blood erupted and floated through the air. It was almost beautiful. Cochineal blood soaked through Danny Boy's shirt where the bullet lay inside his flesh. His hand was curled against his stomach, a useless photograph of carnage.

Bending down, The Ghost ripped off the apron. He opened Danny's bloody shirt. Danny's heart pounded a jungle rhythm in his chest, and the thumps of his pulse sent shockwaves into the atmosphere. His heels of his kid boots kicked the dirt in pain.

The old man lumbered to his knees. His son's body whistled with gunshot wounds.

His boy was a dead man, and there was absolutely nothing he could do about it.

Pulling the shamrock out of the fire, the glow of the iron looked menacing. The Ghost studied the orange, pulsing iron. Heat radiated through it like a heartbeat. He knelt down toward Danny and jammed the hot iron into the criminal's chest.

Danny's eyes grew wide, making the whites look cartoonish. The hiss of the shamrock seared his flesh, providing acres more pain than the bullet ever could. The old man watched his son in terrible, gut-wrenching torture.

"For my brother, I want you to know what suffering's like. While his body was on fire, someone put a bullet in his head. You'll suffer, and you'll die for the hurt you've caused my family and whoever else along the way." He looked over to the struggling old man.

"Paw, don't go getting brave. You ain't savin' your sorry son's hide."

The father stood, and lumbered toward his son and his aggressor. Trying not to kill him, The Ghost took a shot and hit his right hip. The blood squirted out, for the split second frozen in the air, it was a perfect cherry stem, hovering. It's opulent beauty lasted for fractions of a second till it fell to the ear floor and atop the stinky rawhide. The old man dropped.

The Ghost lifted the iron off Danny Boy. Skin stuck as he pulled. Danny's yelp satisfied him.

Outside, people gathered and gossiped. Soon, the law would arrive.

"Danny, you got a choice. I can torture you till you stop breathing. Or I can put you out of your misery." The Ghost said. He lit a cigarillo and stuck it on his bottom lip. He crouched low, so he heard Danny.

The brand looked horrific. Danny's flesh festered black. It would be a gift to die.

The Ghost crept in, six inches from Danny's face. He could smell the sweat and charred flesh. "Way I see it, you provide me with information and we'll be square." The Ghost poked his finger into the crusty, blood black shamrock. Danny howled.

"Die without shame, you pushed the poor old codger over. He's gonna be a cripple for the rest of his life 'cause of you." He flicked some of the charred, ashy skin from the wound. Danny's teeth nearly cracked from the pressure from his clenched jaw. "I ain't a religious man, Danny." The Ghost looked over to the old man writhing in agony. "God's wrath ain't shit to me."

"Your memory best get real good. Tell me where I can find the rest of your posse so they'll get theirs. I'll give you a clean shot. This'll be over."

The pool of blood surrounding Danny grew. The stench of copper seeded the air with vicious tendrils. The sweat on his brow beaded further, his breathing became labored. His memories of the heinous crimes they committed flashed through him; the dynamite explosion to the side of a train, the bodies spilled into the dirt. The squeeze of his trigger, killing without remorse, the devil knew Danny Boy and would collect on his soul.

Pushing the air out of his lungs, he offered one last sentence.

"New Orleans." And with a final push, the life escaped Danny Boy McKay. His dead eyes were open.

The Ghost drug his fingers across Danny Boy's eyelids, closing them. The Ghost dusted himself off and looked out toward the street. People stood along porches, close enough to whisper, but far enough away to avoid bullets.

He flicked the cigarillo toward a puddle of horse piss and waited for the Sheriff to come. He saw the posse of men riding up with their shotguns raised; it wouldn't be the first time someone assumed he was the villain.

SNAKE EYES

No one missed Danny Boy. No friends or kin sought revenge. No boozed up, whiskey-breathed cowboys stumbled through the wooden doors, calling out for The Ghost. Danny Boy wasn't a man of the town's heart. As far as The Ghost knew, not a single soul visited his bullet-ridden husk at the undertaker's parlor. The old man died in his sleep two days following. Be it broken bones or a broken heart, the life inside escaped him. The McKay family line dried up like a creek bed in a blistering summer heat. The Ghost felt a pang of sadness for the old coot, watching his boy die.

When the sheriff and his posse jumped from their horses, their gun barrels pointed at The Ghost's head, they approached him with caution. After presenting the proper papers, the sheriff called the posse off. Facts were facts.

Six to go.

《《《 — 》》》

New Orleans was next. If it was a wild goose chase, then so be it, but he had the suspicion Danny Boy wanted to see his

47

friends hang just the same. If crisscrossing the territories and uncovering each of those dog-faced bastards was what it took, he'd die trying.

The Shamrock brand was up in his room. When it was all over, it would hang above the fireplace. His children's children would know it as a symbol, a ribbon of sacrifice within the family name.

The Ghost stuck around Madrid to let his shoulder heal. Men around town regarded him with a nod or tip of the hat. The criminals coiled up under the rocks, and waited him out, none stupid enough to be impudent and wind up on a slab themselves.

He sipped on a glass of bourbon a few days later, at the far end of the bar in his hotel. Overhead was a battered old painting of a beautiful horse. The frame had been to hell and back, its once golden hue coagulated into a dull yellow vomit after the pounds of dust and cobwebs took their toll on the shine. The painting itself was clean and preserved the soul of the beast. The horse galloped through a vast, emerald prairie. It looked carefree, wild.

His bourbon tasted mighty fine. A small tornado of possibilities spun in front of him. A kaleidoscope of passion and thoughts collided.

Killing Danny Boy was different. Nothing was like this. For ten hard years, he'd traveled each horrendous inch of this America, touching all the land between the two oceans. Penny by penny, he'd made his daily bread collecting the souls. They always fought back. He'd gotten used to never bringing anyone in alive. Why rot in a jail cell to get a noose when going out like a true outlaw was how the real cowboys did it? Dying with your boots on meant honor, and no one would take that away from a man in his final hour. The Ghost sought out the worst of the worst and collected the heads of those who'd sooner fight over matchsticks to the end than ever be in front of a windbag judge.

The Ghost wanted the worst. The thrill of those hunts, the psychological chess matches never got old. Moving his pieces around the board, he fulfilled a void within.

He took a long swallow of the hooch. His eyes grew heavy with drink, a solemn brightness illuminated through him, even though he appeared no sharper than a man burying his mother to the naked eye.

The black fellow behind the bar poured him a tall one, liquid spilling to the rim. And as The Ghost made the attempt to pull out a few coins to pay for the new drink, the barkeep walked away, not giving him the satisfaction of payment. The Ghost's money was no good to him.

Danny Boy, a known bigot, continually refused the colored man's status as free. He insisted, "No nigger could have his shamrock anywhere near his monkey ass," when the barkeep inquired about a saddle for his horse. Danny Boy pondered aloud, leaning with his elbows on the bar top, facing toward a small group of onlookers, "How could a two-legged, black beast ride a four-legged beast? A myth I guess. Ain't no coon ridin' with my good name near his black ass. And that's a fact." The bartender never forgot those words. Danny Boy McKay's recent acquisition of an eternity in a pine box was a small pang of personal revenge. The Ghost was a muted hero to someone he didn't know, and for reasons uglier than anything he took up with.

The Ghost sat with his new glass, and his world spun. He drifted to a story his father used to bring up. How when he and Daniel were boys, they traveled to the Hot Springs in Arkansas. They went to see an old Indian. Their mother was sick with constant fevers and headaches and with a fear of the consumption rampant, their father ponied up his sons and set out for Arkansas. The legend of this wise, old medicine man spread throughout hundreds of miles. Folks from all corners said he could cure anything.

Getting council with him wasn't easy. It took patience and respect for the native people who were here long before any pale-faced bastard with a sense of false entitlement. The elder Masterson was no dummy, and growing up when the Indians were decimated for their scalps in a sickening land grab, he understood common courtesy.

While the natives in the area were known for ruthlessness, the Quapaw remained docile in the face of constant white threat. Riding into the town, the Mastersons were lead to the edge of the bubbling spring. The water fizzed and popped, with a gentle steam rising off the top; the natives viewed it as sacred. People rode from afar to bathe in the healing waters, and the old man was the sole spiritual protector of the area. No one came near the hot springs without his blessing.

Their guide led them to the village. The smell of grilled meat hung in the air while people spoke a strange language. Their father ponied up a considerable amount to be here. The local natives looked them over in passing; the dirty-faced children played with the bones of the buffalo, chasing one another in childish games. No one said anything to the two small white boys lost in the red man's encampment.

The young native spoke clear English and brought them to see the old shaman, whose makeshift doctor's office showed no signs of wealth. It was a roughshod teepee littered with hides and piles of bones.

A rise of smoke trickled out the top, and as their father entered the domain with the young guide, the two boys were instructed to wait outside. They heard a variety of chanting and shaking of mysterious amulets.

Long moments passed, and boredom took over, so the boys explored the so-called "medicinal waters." Not understanding the prowess of the springs, they played like any other children, throwing rocks and sticks into the sacred springs.

When their father finished with the ancient shaman, the three men exited, and drank in the scene of tranquility before them. The section of the forest was quiet. Father held a small package that promised to shake the devil out of his wife and restore her to full health.

As the three men embraced in official goodbyes, Masterson Sr. looked over, and both sons were pissing into the medicinal waters. Looking over to the old Indian, the father was speechless, fearing outrage. The ancient man offered a toothless grin and patted the father on the shoulder. He whispered something to his young interpreter before walking into his abode. The old man laughed. The father faced the younger Indian.

"He says it's ok. The waters feel nice, but it's a bunch of bullshit."

The Ghost soaked in the memory. The same drunkard piano player hacked up the keys, this time murdering a song resembling Chopin.

The Ghost eyed a whore who couldn't escape him. Her eyes sucked him into a vortex. He felt her grow closer without moving an inch. Dressed to the tilt in the sexiest get up this side of Paris, it was a damn shame she rotted away in this one-horse shithole.

He wasn't about to pay 10% of his earnings to taste her French perfume. The world is full of beautiful girls, and all the peripheral looks were free of charge. The whore made eyes. The Ghost tipped a silent cheers toward her and threw back his liquor.

She seethed from across the room at his boldness. No matter what slack-jawed John she pretended to chat up, her smoky eyes slithered to him. He focused his attention toward the drink. Frustrated, she dropped beside him.

"Well?" she demanded.

"Well, what? I'm minding my own. You sauntered over here."

"You ain't gonna talk to me?"

"Not wasting my breath. You're nothing but trouble. Could tell from a country mile." The Ghost was tipsy. His devil may care attitude incensed her. Men fell to her feet in this awful place. He shrugged his shoulders, offering her nothing. Right now, she hated him. Grabbing his glass, she swallowed everything.

"Hey! That was mine—I ain't buying you any drinks. This ain't my first rodeo."

With a nod of her head, two fresh glasses sat in front of them. The bartender beamed with pride. He was happy to see his man winning.

"There. You've gotta fresh drink and a new friend. I'm Charlotte."

"Well, ain't you a flower picked from the sweetest fields the world has ever seen." He lifted his glass upwards, a little spilled across his knuckles. "Ms. Charlotte. Call me Ghost," he said, oozing with sarcasm. She eyed him over.

He wasn't like her clientele, who begged for her, pawed at her. This man paid her no mind, and it drove her mad.

"I been watching you. Everyone has."

"That a fact?"

"Sure as shit is. You killt Danny Boy. Far as I'm concerned you're a fuckin' hero."

"Just providing a service to mankind."

"Whatever you say." Charlotte laid her eyes upon him, catlike and smoldering. "You made the Sheriff look awful silly. Claims he had no idea Danny Boy was a killer. Too bad everyone in town knew he was a fucking dog."

"I'm outta here at first light. No time to learn Danny's local history."

"That a fact? You going looking for more blood?" she purred. She liked men with a powerful, violent streak. His nonchalance for murder turned her on. He didn't rely on his gun but wasn't afraid to use it. In a world like this, a good, hard man got rarer by the minute.

"None clearer." The Ghost answered. A slick chemistry brewed. A strange palpitation fluttered.

"Aren't you afraid his posse will band up and come looking for you after what you did? One man can't kill the world."

"I weren't ever Danny Boy's girl. I didn't like the way his eyes looked. He scared me. I'm damn sure he killed my best girlfriend, Sassy. She used to run oft with him now and again, and one day she wound up in a gulley with her neck slit. I know he killt her. I just know it."

"I know you know how to shoot a gun. Seem like the type. You coulda taken him out yourself. Shit, coulda had one of your boyfriends do it."

"Who in all of shit is gonna defend a whore? I ain't nothin' but somewhere to throw a fuck. My friend's still dead. You did the world a favor. I know you got your reasons, but those ain't my concern."

She leaned in closer, trying to catch the fresh aftershave smell. He took schoolboy glances at the flesh oozing out of the top of her bustier.

"I reckon I appreciate the kindness. I ain't looking for company. You're welcome for the service."

"This ain't a business call. Calm your horses. We're just chattin'. Whatchu gonna do when this is all over? Way I see it you like your job."

"Used to like the job. Nowadays I just want quiet. If I could go without hearing the sound of a gunshot, it'd make me happier than horseshit."

"Don't sound like no fun," she said, rubbing her leg against his.

"I've had all the fun a man could want. I've seen things that'd make your hair go white."

"I'm a whore; I seen plenty. More than you'll know. We don't get much respect you know."

"Glad we're having a pissing contest."

Charlotte's eyes smoldered with anger.

"You don't scare me. You may be iron fuckin' cored, and full of scars. I see hurtin' in you. You wouldn't hurt a soul if it wasn't without purpose. I admire that. I can tell a decent man when I see one. I sit here day in and day out. I see loads of men and few of them ain't much better than a regular ole' hound. It hurt my heart for a long time. Knowin' Danny Boy is dead gives me peace. So take your holier than thou attitude and shove it up your fuckin' ass. Ya hear?"

The Ghost pursed his lips and motioned for her to be served. Taking a second to process his alcohol, and the return of the exquisite harlot, he chose his words.

"Thanks for the vote of confidence. Danny Boy got his. It was well deserved. But, honey I ain't looking for a business relationship. So, you'd best move on than expect to make any money sitting here with my sorry ass. When I finish this here drink, I'm off to bed."

"Who in Christmas shit said I'm trying to make a buck? Look, friend, if I want what's in them breeches, I'm taking it."

The Ghost remembered his sister in law and his niece. At how they too, died because of Danny Boy's inner hatred for women. He was a hanger-on, by all accounts. No way would anyone cum after him. Forget sloppy seconds, and filthy fifths, he was last out of seven.

Sweat beaded, and her breasts rose and fell. Her skin tingled with lust. The Ghost was no boy and for these few moments, she wanted to be near him; to crawl inside of him, to soak in the warmth he radiated. His coldness was for the killers of men, and for the scoundrels and rats. Charlotte saw him as a loving daddy, or a man tipping a cent into the hat of the down on their luck. In her mind, he was a desperado poet, a specter walking amongst the bright, luminous rays of a childish pastel fantasy. He was a man she could cling on to.

Men with skeletons in their closets cast long shadows, The Ghost's shadow cast for lifetimes. Let her have the fantasy.

She'd had plenty of run-ins with curs like Danny Boy, and as the local law thought her and other working girls as nothing less than a place to park their cocks for a few minutes, she knew death was one gunshot, or overdose away.

The right side of her bed remained cold, and she held out for a man to share it who wouldn't hurt or haunt her. One who wouldn't beg for the unreasonable or promise acres of lies; he was a man she wanted to kiss on the mouth.

"Get off your stool. You're taking me to your room."

"I ain't paying for company."

"That's why we ain't headed to my room. I'm *your* guest. Swallow what's in your glass."

The Ghost looked at the long pull sitting at the bottom half of the glass. Murky and brown, it taunted his liver. He slammed the glass, and then pulled out a wad of coins and paper money. He peeled off a few large bills and left more than enough to cover the tabs for the entire night. Small thanks for the kindness.

"Let's go."

«« — »»

He was off before the first light. Charlotte, the bartender, and the rest of Madrid slept in eerie small town silence as he rode into the complete blackness beyond borders. Packing an extra blanket and effects for at least seven days worth of traveling east, he was ready to find the next card to fall. The sliver of the moon looked frozen in the air. It appeared like a scythe, a reminder of the purpose of the journey.

The Ghost pulled the wool of his collar up, shielding skin from the elements. The chill in the air wrapped itself around him and froze the blood flowing inside. The steam rose from the nostrils of Chalky as he trampled through the shale and sediment. East Texas was filled with plenty of foliage and sources of water, unlike its western counterpart. The travel to New Orleans wouldn't be as bad as a few journeys in the past.

Darkness embraced and far off into the distance, he saw the dying embers of campfires from whatever band of thugs, cowboys or Indians. Riding during the dark hours was the best way to slink around. The night was how you secured a kill. No one expects it when they're sleeping. Even if one stood watch, they dozed off. People tried to remain prepared in the event of a night attack, but a man needs slumber. Unless the door locks, the world is stocked with predators.

Once, he tracked a man through the unforgiving deserts of Arizona. It was a dangerous, long haul, and fraught with unbearable heat in the day, and frigid desert nights. Men were prone to burying themselves in the sand, hoping to retain body heat if they didn't want to make a fire and risk being seen.

The American Southwestern desert, a barren wasteland littered with the whitewashed bones of victims to the elements, or of the Indians who knew how to prey on those unaccustomed to the dry song of the sand. The man The Ghost hunted was wanted across Georgia and Alabama. A low-down ornery villain with a vicious streak for killing the patrons of banks after he'd robbed them.

His name was Sebastian Glit. One shot, one kill; Glit was a sniper for the Confederacy, and his short range was better than his decorated distance shots.

After the war had ended, he'd never found his place in society. The anger inside brewed and bubbled, creating a killer.

No longer was Glit a man celebrated for his victories in death; he was the hunted.

The Ghost tracked him to an encampment up around the Navajo Territory. He was far out of his comfort zone. He assumed fleeing west he'd be scot-free. He'd start the process over once they rode into a town worth taking. Faulty dreams.

Glit, and two other brown-toothed degenerates he'd picked up somewhere slept under a frozen moon and distant stars. The Ghost studied them from afar. Loading his rifle, his eyes watched these men enjoy their last moments of serenity.

A man so wanted, idly slept without defense. Yards away, his killer stalked. Poetic justice. In death, Glit would appreciate how he was taken down; it was fair. He slept free and simple. Men looked less like animals through a set of crosshairs.

The side of Glit's head exploded. His brains splashed the two sleeping men. Both jumped out of their skin, each with their fingers on their pistols, their eyes wild and feral. The mud color of their teeth glared against the flames of the fire. Like stupid men do, they laid blame on one another. Arguing who done it, each of the simpletons blasted in a fury of fear. They'd executed one another over nothing. They did The Ghost's job for him. He'd cash in on the back of stupidity. Times like this didn't happen enough: $200—easy money for one squeeze of the trigger.

He rode down and examined the area. Glit and his boys had quite the haul; plenty of guns, blankets and food. He'd load the corpse up on the back of his horse and drop the festering pile of shit off at the sheriff's and collect big. Examining Glit's body, The Ghost saw something he'd only heard rumors of. On Glit's neck was a Hog's Tooth.

While men are decorated for their actions in the field, a sharpshooter received praise for his ability to kill at a distance. But, there was one trophy a sharp shooter desired above all others: the bullet of the man who was hunting him. Every military sect relies on someone with a keen eye off in the distance. Once in a great while, two of those hidden assassins catch one another in the cross hairs.

Might against iron will: someone hunting their enemy for the same reasons. To take the life of another like you was romantic and chaotic, beautiful and sacred. These moments were the white buffalo.

Examining the relic, The Ghost held the life of a man boiled down to a simple object. Finality stamped its name in the iron core. He studied the bullet and imagined Glit saddled up on a hill picking off the enemy. Looking down the barrel of his gun, who comes into view but his equal on the other side?

Two men stare into their crosshairs, letting the dance begin. Glit saw him first and pulled the trigger. With one shot, he erased his equal. It was the ultimate honor to own your killer's bullet.

The Ghost tied the stark reminder around his neck. He'd blasted off part of an ex-sharp shooter's head. He took a minute to let it settle, and then gathered up what remained of the two useless bodies and burned them. The flames rose high into the night air. The stench of searing flesh stunk for miles. He'd haul Glit into the next town and cash in on another dead man's head: business as usual.

《《《 — 》》》

The miles in pursuit of Snake Eyes accrued underfoot of the tired Chalky. They listened to the symphony of the forest writhe and howl like the gears of a working machine.

There was a strong sense of purpose continuing east toward Louisiana. The thick cedar scent of East Texas intoxicated the senses while the acres of staggering floral beauty enraptured him. Soon, the flowers would erupt into a volcano of vibrant reds, and cool blues within the sea of green in the long fields.

They stopped at a small creek for a drink. Crystal clear water glided over the worn rocks. The water was frigid, and splashing it across his skin, the brightness of temperature lit his skin afire with a rigid prick. They drank till their bellies were full with fresh, un-molested water. The Ghost gave his four-legged companion a good scratch behind the ears.

Continuing down into a low-slung valley, the world opened up. Lush grasses stood knee-high, and the sunflowers rose into the sky, operating as a landing pad for a fantastic array of winged creatures. Out here in the wilds of the natural world, a man was a speck in the vast openness. He felt insignificant passing through tree-lined canyons and dipping into high fields with swaying tall grass.

Lost in the sea of green, The Ghost and Chalky passed a ravaged doe carcass. The festering scent and rotting black blood stunk to high hell. Someone cleaned bones of meat and salvageable parts, to white man standards.

The local tribes would have never left a deer in this haphazard condition. There was too much sustenance still left to offer, and the white man that slayed her never knew the potential he pissed away.

The scavengers took turns cleaning and pillaging meat left on the bones within the last two or three days. Greasy parts of flesh hung off the skull. Portions of teeth exposed, snarling white against the gore. The sun shone into the eyeless sockets. The hooves were filthy from the struggle, and blood caked on in thick layers. Two massive vultures swooped in, dropping upon the body, crushing the doe's fragile bones with their enormity. Macabre cries echoed into the hills, fighting for a morsel of rotten organ meat.

Their long black wings flapped like ominous shadows while feasting on the vanquished herbivore. Their claws dug into the remaining guts while their beaks shined cherry.

Certain darkness crept through the landscape. The devil's cape blackened all it touched. The trees grew long like dinosaur tails, and the moss hung like a death shroud while the water remained inches under the soil beneath the boots.

Miles passed, The Ghost trailed off from the stable grounds of Texas and into the confused deities populating Louisiana.

The Ghost rode high along the ridgelines, and he rode smart. Between the constant threat of attack from the swamp-dwelling Indians, the land itself was unforgiving, and would kill anyone who wasn't born atop the murky waters. From gators to coons and little cats who'd rip your throat out with a quick swipe, it was best to avoid such a place unless a man had a guide or a death wish.

They came to a narrow river that stretched for miles in either direction. He'd crossed it a few times over the years, and it was always a bitch. The water was freezing. It would lay a chill deep into his bones the second he was inside the flowing beast. Getting in, he hissed. It was hypothermia territory despite the pounding heat on land; Luckily the water wasn't so deep, a little less than waist high. He kept everything above his head, especially his rifle and pistols. Half way through the murky expanse, he heard a mighty bellow. On the other side of the river was a massive creature, dwarfed only by God himself. An enormous black bear howled. The great natural monster stood tall on his hind legs. The Ghost held one of the revolvers and took aim should the bear come closer.

The bear belted another roar. The great animal's eyes locked on the flesh of The Ghost and his horse. It took swats at the ground while taking long breaths, like sneezes. Chalky tensed up next to him. Veering to the left to establish more room between himself and the great predator, he jerked Chalky out of his state of shock. They paused and found a point where the water was only knee deep. The Ghost placed his saddlebags back over Chalky while keeping aim on the beast.

Broaching land, the massive, rapacious thing bared its teeth, the long strands of saliva hanging from its jowls. The bear howled again. It would crush him and his four-legged companion. The Ghost had no choice but to fight back or die by the bear's claws.

Taking aim at the head, The Ghost pulled the trigger. A bullet smashed into the bone of the bear's face. Bone below the right eye shattered, the bear groaned as the bullet sunk into the flesh, past the fur.

Animals hidden out of sight sniffed the air with ears perked up, curious as to what the strange sound was. The bear still stood. Absolute within its resolve to destroy this man-thing daring to cross into the forbidden zone, the bear waited for his opponent. Blood trickled down its fur; it was on the ready with no deterrent.

The Ghost fired the second shot: this time striking the chest, aiming for the heart. Black blood poured, matting the fur. The great animal's nose tickled the air, taking in the blood-scented breeze dancing ballerina-like. Blood mixed with the wet sand at the water's edge.

Another shot flew out of the barrel, exploding the skull and killing the animal. Its clawed toes relaxed their grip as the life drained from the formidable creature. The blood mixed with the sand.

The Ghost led his horse to land. It trotted and danced, moving away from the corpse. Chalky sensed the spirit of the animal slinking through the azure firmament and didn't want to be near as it took its journey elsewhere. Hopping off, The Ghost pulled out his skinning knife. The knife looked like a witch finger, razor sharp and with a long curve.

The bear meat sizzled as the flames licked the surface of the flesh. It wasn't his finest meal, but damn sure wasn't the worst, either.

He took what he could eat for dinner, and a bit of the road. The rest of the meat was rubbed with salt, preserving what he could for the coming days. His clothes dried on the rocks while he sat naked on his bedroll, thankful for the heat of the fire.

Off in the distance, lobos gathered around the bear corpse. With blood in their fur, they enjoyed the first round of decay. The whites of their eyes and tips of their canines shone under the blood moon hanging the wild night sky. The fire cracked and popped. He looked at the stars and listened to the cacophony of savagery in the wilderness.

For a slight moment, he was content; a feeling that eluded him. The Ghost's body, mind, and ears were tuned to the vibrations of finality as he slept. For the moment, he was at peace.

The sun rose over the tops of the oaks, stabbing his eyelids. Chalky was awake, grazing on nearby grass. The vanquished bear lay off in the distance. The Ghost walked over to check the damage from the night. Vicious jaws took massive deposits of flesh.

Nothing remained of the hunks of meat surrounding the area where he took his cut. The internal organs spilled out, half eaten. Flies buzzed in the thousands while maggots laid their claim.

«« — »»

They approached a clearing where the trees died off for a few miles. The landscape was wide open. A thin wisp of gray smoke rose into the air off in the distance. The closer he rode, the more apparent the horror was. No one moved.

He looked in all directions, his rifle at the ready. Both revolvers were cocked. He stumbled upon a massacre. Dead men hung out of the skeletal remains of what looked like a wagon train headed west. Oxen's necks were slit, defeated in the bloody grass. Pack mule brains splattered the side of the wagons.

Even valuable horses lie with open, dead eyes. Eviscerated bodies lay in a tangled, violent mess off to the sides while countless arrows stuck out of the wood from missed shots. Bodies and blood strewn about like a blanket coming apart at the seams.

The pungent stench of death lingered in the air. Headless corpses mingled with others who missed hands or feet. Men lie in crumpled messes. Women's bodies were slashed to ribbons, entrails, and viscera thrown like a New Year's celebration. Tragic trophies were taken. Dark blood stained the weathered wood of the wagon trains. Women and children lay out upon large rocks with crushed faces snarling up at God for the fate they suffered.

Gone was the ease he'd felt last night. He stood over the body of an eyeless child; he stared into her rotten eye sockets, her hair matted with dried blood. This was a celebration of madness. This was Comanche territory, and the warriors of blood wanted to make a statement. Only the devil himself could imagine such great hideousness.

The Ghost rode onward as the eyes of the dead watched him fade under a shining sun.

«« —— »»

Huge railroad encampments dotted the country all with the common goal of ending up at the Pacific coast, and as each piece of steel accrued into lengthy miles, a new America was born. No longer did folks want to live and die in their backyard.

The national rift was sealed with a threadbare bandage. The war was long over, but the ghosts from the Battle for America haunted every inch of the nubile, stolen land.

Before he was a bounty hunter, The Ghost had a Christian name; he was a part of the living world.

That life died with his comrades in the struggle—he was a sharp shooter for the Union Army. After the violence, he became a man with no name, an entity to be known by; while countless men lost limbs or lives, he lost his humanity. Neither side benefitted from the deaths of their brothers, friends, and comrades. Now, on wanted posters across the land, men who only knew violence did nothing but beg for more of their pained ailment of gunsmoke and cruelty.

Many servicemen who fought on the Confederate side became jaded with the new America. They banded up and became the cowboys or rustlers of terror. The tragic American dream of a man without a home led to those making a living thieving, killing and forming the outlaw gangs. Men felt robbed of their wills.

By men's bad choices, he was given a chance at a new career. The colors between the black and white of law and villainy were a charcoal gray, at best.

Killing the killer was easier than trying to bring him to trial. Justice lived in many forms, but the most practical was the end of the gun.

Bands of apathetic men robbed the railroads, the mills, and most of all: the banks. The America they fought for back in the war didn't exist, and by robbing the people who funded the war in the first place, those on the other side of the law, felt above it while counting their caches of dollar bills. The argument for the soul of the union was nothing but a myth.

The land closed in and the trees flooded. The forests of East Texas swallowed life in oaks and pine. He was within reach of his special hiding place.

Unless you knew the markings or the signs of its existence, you'd pass it right up. He always holed up there when he passed through this area. He'd been using it as a cover for years; they'd discovered it by accident as his regimen was headed to Texas following Appomattox. They'd slept here on their way to deal with the Mexicans south of the border. Ever since, this was his ace in the hole. He was near Neuville, Texas, a sleepy blink of a town. He stopped at the local trading post and bought bullets and bacon, a fair trade for the bear's flesh.

The cave was a long hallway with one right arm twist, blocked by a large tree. The entryway was high enough to walk the horse through, should it want to come inside. He made his fire at the entrance and tossed the rest of the bear meat in with the bacon. The two types of meat coalesced and as the bear meat danced in the pork grease; the mixture was intoxicating. He took a few nips from his whiskey bottle and listened to the wind and the hiss of the fire.

This was freedom. He'd sleep sound in his cave of solitude. The Ghost had no masters and owed nothing to no man. Despite the scars and the slashes, the bar fights, and the bullet holes in his clothes, this was all he knew.

There was a sense of satisfaction when crossing a name off the Wanted list. When he put that bullet into Colm Beattie's head, it felt like every scream of agony from a mother's breast guided his bullet. Knowing that corpse laid on ice while the local undertaker dug rudimentary tool through the dead flesh felt right.

The Ghost looked at his hands and went through the timeline of scars, none of them felt like a burden or a mistake, but a map of a life that was beautiful in the most tragic sense. Owning one's burden separates the dreamers and badmen from the angels of absolution and the divine music of retribution.

«« — »»

He reached New Orleans after three days. When he made it to town, he took in the vast clashes of fidelity and enjoyed seeing the everyday world dumped on its head. New Orleans didn't operate like the rest of America. He'd spent enough time here to know the status quo was a mirage.

The sun shone against the top of the highest spire of St. Louis Cathedral, beckoning him as a welcomed friend. Men sat in open-air bars arguing, laughing in flavors of language. He smelled the spilled beer riding past the pirate Laffite's musky place on Bourbon's far end. He hadn't been back through town since putting Elbridge in a pine box but was it nice.

The sound of the ferries and the freighters hummed as their husky whistles rang heavy like the moisture in the air. In this wonderfully chaotic place, a maestro played the hell out of the calliope, and its bright tones reminded The Ghost of the better parts of his dreams. Here, he was a stranger amongst strangers.

The most notorious killer of the entire city lay in front of him: The Mississippi River. Many fell in after an evening with the bottle or a whore with a blade. When the substantial weight of a body splashed into the water, the undertow would wrap its arms around and low low below they'd go. The great killer glistened in the sunlight as the water crashed in small waves at the shoreline. A soundtrack of seabirds cawed, diving for scraps of waste fishermen threw in after cleaning catch.

Two dock workers unloaded barrels of shrimp while arguing with each other. Names were called, and challenges issued. Their eyes locked and within seconds an argument became a promise: who bluffed and who was serious?

A barrel fell to its side, and the argument became uproar. Knives were pulled. The rest of the dock stopped work. The silent dance began. They moved in a slow circle. The larger of the two men didn't trust his instincts. Panic. He knew he'd crossed the line. No longer was this a petty bullshit fight; it was real. The smaller man had dark, feral eyes. His mouth was agape, showing horrid, umber dental work hanging inside his jaw. His knuckles pressed ivory against the handle of his blade. His vapid face wanted death. No more belittling ever again. With a great leap, his blade slid into the stomach of the larger man. The bigger man slept on the anger of the smaller, and he'd paid the price for his slow reaction time.

The small man's wrist moved across the belly, spilling the contents of the large man's GI tract. The whites of the large man's eyes grew massive as his guts poured on his boot tops. The smaller man wiped the blood off his blade on his pant leg and closed his knife. He cleaned up the spilled shrimp. The large man lay in a pool and bled.

The crowd who'd watched the commotion returned to their business, paying no fewer minds to a child selling shoe shines or newspapers.

After the man had died, urchins picked him clean of valuables. His body went into the river, where it sank. Another moment in a city founded by pirates and maintained by the corrupt.

New Orleans was a different animal than the one-horse towns of the building scrum on the western front. While he enjoyed New Orleans desires, The Ghost knew winding up in a shallow grave was too easy in the Crescent City.

Cowboys watched their ass in these parts. For as hard as any frontiersman could be, they knew nothing of these streets, blood flowed beneath the pavement in this town.

New Orleans, the genesis of this whole blood-soaked manhunt; the city founded by pirates and established in blood, sweat and lies; the town that never sleeps because it's waiting for the grim reaper. The drunks were meaner around here; they'd kill you with anything in arm's reach. Built on the broken backs of many men of many social and cultural variations, New Orleans is the scar-faced whore with nothing to lose. She's already given your heart intimacy; she wanted your soul in return.

A crew of banditos couldn't roll into town and shoot up the joint like out west. The worst of the worst held his hat when dwelling within the confines of somewhere so grim, the violence and massacre impregnated each inch of phosphorous slate.

«« — »»

He sat in a musky little bar at the end of the French Quarter. It was quaint and quiet. He pulled out a cigarillo and held the flame of a candle sitting on the bar top toward the end. The flame married the tobacco and smoke was born. He took in a long drag. As the smoke escaped from his mouth, he looked at the bartender. He studied him. After one or two glasses of poison, the bartender smiled half-heartedly, feeling the man in black stare at him. The bartender was about to explode by the time The Ghost spoke up.

"'Scuse me, was deliberating if you might provide me with some information." He didn't form it as a question but as a statement.

"I'm hearin' the proposition. Who or what ya lookin' fer?" The bartender answered, coming closer. He was senior to The

Ghost by ten years. His aura of ease and decency illuminated The Ghost immediately.

The Ghost took a long drag, and then took the shot of whiskey in front of him. When he was done with the shot, he exhaled the smoke.

"Looking for some people, or maybe just a feller. Can't say. Heard someone was in town through the grapevine."

The bartender wiped his mug slower. He raised an eyebrow with skepticism, as if what he'd been asked made no sense. It was almost like a jigsaw puzzle or brainteaser. When subjects like this arose it was best to walk the line in case of chaos.

"At all depends, friend. I knows plentya folks. People come 'n go, though. So, might not be any help. At said, in certain situations I'm always looking to make a few bucks, dependin' on who's asking."

The Ghost unfolded the wanted poster he kept in his coat pocket. The six remaining members of The Red Seven gang sneered while Danny Boy had a large X drawn through his face.

The poster read:

WANTED!
The kill or capture of
The Red Seven Gang.

Wanted by the United States Federal Government for multiple train and bank robberies, and the murder of innocents. The United States of America seeks the imprisonment of these offenders. A bounty will be paid upon proof their capture.

DEAD OR ALIVE.

A crude drawing of each man was featured next to his name, or what the law had to go on for his known aliases. Listed were partial names, and nicknames, or any information available.

Listed below the announcement were their faces and names.

"Snake Eyes" Ed Taylor
Danny Boy McKay
Desalvo Cortez
Phineas Alexander
Charley War Chief
Red "The Fixer" Montague
Hidalgo Montoya

"Looking for these here men. Killed one of 'em already." He looked the bartender straight in the eyes. The talk wasn't cheap. "My money's on the man they call Snake Eyes. His Christian name's Ed Taylor. Ol' Ed's a native. Fore' I go asking around town, you may be able to make life easier."

He pulled silver bits out of his pocket and slid them toward the bartender. It was more money than the bartender made in the last two days.

"Need more? I got it."

"Feller, if yer pushing this kinda money my way on a maybe, yew must want to see this man real bad." The bartender replied.

"I ain't here to make friends."

"At's sure as shit. If you killed one'em already. Seems yer mind's deadset."

"If you can help me out, I'll triple this." The Ghost's finger jammed the top of the silver coin. The bartender licked his lips. The stranger's gravedark eyes sat like two floating black orbs beneath the long, sable brim of his hat.

"Suppose you ain't a preacher dressed like that."

"No ghosts, no God. I'm here to kill Ed Taylor."

The bartender paused on the beat of the new information presented.

"Know of a man?"

"I'm on terms with the local undertaker. His name's Ed. He's rumored to have a checkered past. He's a Grayback if it makes any difference to yew. I served under Lee n took a few bullets. We've got to talkin' a spell or two. We ain't close or nothin'.

Don't fuss much, though. Why you fixing to hurt this man? Fore' I give ye any real information on 'im, I need ta know why a man lookin' like he's crawled out from the grave's here looking fer a feller who's alright in my book."

"His name is on a Wanted poster. That ain't enough?" The Ghost asked.

"Friend, I've known plenty of good men whose name's were on a Wanted poster."

"I got personal business. Taylor did my kin wrong: murdered my brother, killed his family. Raped my niece and brother's wife. Who'd want to harbor a man who's raped and killed a little girl?"

The bartender eyed him. He wasn't a dolt and wasn't in the presence of a liar looking to capitalize on nefarious business. Playing the stranger straight was in his best interest. Dying over a man he wasn't close with wasn't worth it.

"No sir. I ain't in league with no man who'd hurt a child, let alone kill one. I'm sorry for your loss. By the looks of yew, I can tell yew'n seen yer fair share of hell, too. I ain't gonna get mixed up in anything sinister?"

The Ghost pointed at the Wanted poster again. His fingertip thumped the wood of the bar. The bartender's eyes scanned the crudely drawn faces while studying the names on the list. Next, The Ghost unfolded a stack of letters for the kill or capture from one honorable judge G. Nazarko of Texas.

The bartender looked at the coins again. The money could be a huge help.

The bartender spilled his guts. "The Ed Taylor I knows is real tall. Damn near seven foot. Thin as a rail, starvin' skinny. Hair's so blond it's colorless. Got real light blue eyes, too. Looks like he's from a diff'rent world. Wears this odd, dirty snow colored suit makes him look like a crumpled up page from the bible.

He's a strange looking bird." The Ghost nodded in recognition. "The nickname yew got for 'im, Snake Eyes— makes sense to me. Got a small pair of eyes tattooed on his left booger hook like a sailor would.

Like, if he's covering his eyes from the sun, the extra set of eyes is lookin' out too. His leg is busted, so he walks with a cane."

"That it?"

The bartender nodded. The Ghost pulled out a black notebook full of scribbles. He wrote down everything.

"I make notes. I get everything in order before I pull the trigger."

The bartender refilled the glass of beer. He stabbed a few chips of ice from the icebox and dropped them into the glass.

"Taylor goes fer a drink 'round the corner from his place. Napoleon's Rose. Small spot. Where all the real low-down boozehounds go. Yew can get a whore around there fer a drink if they don't cut your liver out first. An opium den's in the back. One thing obvious from a country mile is Ol' Ed loves him, China White. He's always high."

"You said he's an undertaker?" The Ghost inquired, writing in his little black book. Many names of dead men lie inside the tattered pages of his little bible.

"Yessir. He got on with one of the old Italian families a while back. They been here a few generations, and 'fore anyone knew it, Taylor was runnin' the joint."

"His place close to here?" The Ghost asked.

"Ahyep. Got a building near Rampart. White-lookin' corner lot. Donletta & Taylor is the name of it these days."

The Ghost pulled out a wad of currency and slid a few dollars toward the bartender. The bartender palmed the cash, and it went in his shirt pocket. His face wasn't one of elated joy; it was one of consternation and sadness.

"Why you look so blue? Thought you and this scum weren't compadres?"

"It ain't that. I never sent a man up the river 'fore. I offered a perfect stranger his head on a platter. I'm supposed to feel right?"

The bartender's eyes brimmed with Christian moral pain. He was an honest man with a good heart. His intentions were in the right place.

"You saw the poster. I told you what he'd done. My brother set afire, burned to death. His boy? Shot in the head. My sister-in-law and niece were raped and killed by these men. They painted a seven on my brother's door in blood." The Ghost said as his finger jabbed the wanted poster.

The bartender held out his hand and looked The Ghost dead in the eye.

"Name's Simon. Walter Simon. This's my place. I live above it. Don't got any kin, just a daughter who survived her momma. It breaks my heart thinkin' of my child as your brother's. Yew need me for anything, come knockin'. We'll sort out whatever yer lookin' for."

"They call me The Ghost."

"I ain't even gonna ask why."

"You're better off."

«« — »»

The Ghost was ready. He'd cleaned up and enjoyed the solace of his hotel room. The room was nice. It had a wall of gold leafed rococo wallpaper sparkling against the flicker of the flame inside the table lamp. A comfortable shade of darkness cast over the space. He felt at home. The Ghost sat at the edge of the bed dressed his undershirt and suspenders. He was deep in the details of cleaning and reloading all of his guns.

Entering Napoleon's Rose, he took a seat at the bar off in the corner. He kept to himself and hovered over his drink. The place was the bottom of the barrel as Simon promised. A perfect place if you were a man like Ed Taylor: a career thief, killer and gambler cum morgue owner?

It made perfect sense: a king amongst the rats. Even the flickering flames trapped within the icy glass of the lamps glowed with a seedy iridescence in this place.

The Ghost eyed the door. He'd been in opium dens before. The flat, foggy smell of the room and the closed-in quarters made one who wasn't high feel claustrophobic.

Years ago, he'd taken a tip a man he hunted was big into the shit. A killer out of Mesa, Arizona, a shameless plug of a man with no soul; The Ghost took eradicating him as a mission, not for God, but the divinity of the living world.

The man had a reckless passion for murdering the Chinese, who worked on the railroads or started little shops in the boomtowns. Little was known about the origin of his racial hatred, but the scores of dead Chinamen spoke loud and clear. As people across the pond had heard of Jack The Ripper, this raccoon-eyed shadow roamed The West, carving up anyone with almond shaped eyes and black hair. The Ghost tracked his target along the California border, near a major encampment of railroad workers. The Chinese parlors of sale and trade followed the miles of track just laid, The Ghost knew to look along their back alleys first.

He paid off the tired Chinese fellow in charge and laid up like the rest of the mind-blown junkies scattered on little couches, eyes half open, and helpless. His man came in looking to get comfortable. The Ghost waited. His target wasn't going anywhere; he had a captive audience tonight. For a short while, the target lay in a comatose state but soon stirred. He moved in the darkness, out of the light of the dim candles. As his target came in for another long suck of the good stuff, he grabbed the barrel of his pursuer's long, black pistol barrel. He took in an extended inward suck. The Ghost pulled the trigger.

It was getting later in the evening when two men stumbled out of the back. Their eyes were tiny fractions. They spoke in whispers. One of the men was a round, hamish slob who'd spent many a penny on large meals.

He looked like a portly politician with a cheap haircut and a cheap suit. His sleepy, blue-grey eyes slithered around the room as he made his way for the door. His movements were molasses-paced, and his psychical motion, laborious. The Asian delights dug its nails into the fat man's brain, and he couldn't comprehend much past breathing.

Traipsing behind the little pig in the suit was an odd man whose hair looked like a pile of snow atop two blue crystals for eyes. He walked with a cane. He appeared much older than expected.

The Ghost crept out of his chair. His cigarillo lay smoldering in the ashtray, his second glass of whiskey untouched.

The pair were a block away before The Ghost made his ascension, the perfect amount of space to catch up before they made it inside the funeral parlor. The two men floated feetless.

The Ghost grew closer. His steps remained light as he tried not to let his boot heels give his position away. The moon hung like a large pie tin while purple clouds slid past at their own, sedate pace.

The Ghost gripped a revolver in each hand. He took a deep breath before hollering toward fate. Both thumbs cocked the hammers on each of his weapons.

"SNAKE EYES ED TAYLOR!"

He could have taken the shot, but that was the coward's way. He wanted Snake Eyes to die knowing who he was. The two men turned around, startled by the yelling behind them.

They knew the cry of a man with a vendetta. Ed Taylor fired a shot licky split. The bullet flew past The Ghost, cutting the air in a bang. The small iron ball crashed into some wooden fencing to his immediate left.

The Ghost took a shot as the two men stirred in disarray; their movements were a low-slung chaotic ballet. His bullet crashed into the lamp above their heads. The crude bullet shattered the glass encasement while silencing the fire trapped inside. He took his time and walked slow. The Ghost fired again. The targets were impaired; this was a hunt, not a slaughter. Trying his hardest to aim, Snake Eyes Ed Taylor swallowed and made his best go at the man in black.

The next bullet from The Ghost's black revolver sank into Taylor's friend. The bullet shattered his knee. The potbellied whale crumpled under the venomous pain of the bullet tearing his flesh. Taylor fired a few shots at The Ghost. His shots were catawampus and cross-eyed.

The Ghost fired off a series of methodical shots. He hit the fat man again. The portly bastard wailed. Taylor, already injured, dropped his cane. He hobbled as fast as his good leg allowed.

Since retiring from The Life, Snake Eyes took an extended sabbatical into the smoky arms of a drug-addled brume. This specter in black floated behind, and despite his efforts, Snake Eyes couldn't hit his target. The Ghost moved quick, like God's hand, moved him from spot to spot. The Ghost fired a bullet, and it nicked the side of Ed Taylor's head. The blood danced through the air in a violent ballet. First blood was drawn.

Taylor fired off another shot toward The Ghost from behind his back. It missed by a country mile. His heart pounded. The Ghost didn't yell or raise a scene. He was a silent enemy; a specter draped in the color of night.

The fat man lie on the ground wheezing; a man in shape would have been able to make a run for it or, at least, fight. The fat bastard bled. The Ghost walked past, ignoring his pained cries. The fellow tried to raise his gun toward The Ghost, but the pig shook from hours inhaling the drugs. His eyes grew to wide white saucers as The Ghost's boot toe connected with his wrist. The fat man's gun went sailing. The pool of blood surrounding him was dark and soaked through his sky blue suit.

The gas lamps flickered behind their glass. The flame throbbed, as violence layered onto the already swampy air. The overhead moon shone bright, offering an ethereal glow to all of the disarray happening on the streets of the French Quarter.

"I have money. Please, take it. Please don't kill me." The fat man pleaded.

"I don't want your money. So shut the fuck up."

The big man clammed up. The Ghost glided past, moving like bars of music in an opera. Picking the fat man's firearm up, The Ghost stuck it in his belt. Just in case he needed more ammo against Snake Eyes.

Turning the corner, he noticed a small relic of irony lying there on the ground. The top of Taylor's cane shone in the moonlight. It was in the likeness of an alligator, the undisputed predator of the swamp. And there were droplets of blood.

〈〈〈 — 〉〉〉

The door to the funeral home was ajar. In Taylor's panic, he must have slammed the door behind, to have it bounce open. The place was nice enough.

It was a large building with stone pillars at either side; less French than it was a mixture of the Spanish influence with a gaudy American flair. A black cast-iron fence surrounded the building while in typical New Orleans fashion the front gate was missing.

The steps leading to the door were worn from many a sad foot walking their dead to the back of a carriage.

The building looked sterile in the moonlight. The Ghost slipped inside; he knew Taylor would be waiting with a shotgun or if he was smart a Gatling gun.

No matter how much adrenaline pumped through Taylor, he'd smoked himself down a few cerebral notches. The Ghost would create chaos to disturb his reality; this was like shooting fish in a barrel.

Swinging inward, he drew ready to fire. Taylor wasn't waiting for him. An eerie quiet lay over the room. The only sound was The Ghost's pulsing heart. The parlor lights were dim, and it took his eyes a second to adjust to the low light. This room was a collector of sadness, a lasting scent of grief copulated with fresh flowers, staining one's reality.

"Snake Eyes Ed Taylor," he shouted. Daring his target to speak up. Another little spatter of blood was on the floor. He was on the path.

"You know why I'm here to kill you. You ain't dumb."

Silence. The Ghost kept his cool while his eyes studied the layout with both guns drawn. The wood below creaked under his weight.

He entered a tight hallway. The main room sat empty save a few scattered chairs, so no place to hide.

A solitary door was to the right. It was solid dark wood, the color of blood. It was locked. He took aim at the lock and fired.

The door swung open. The room was tiny and bare, not large enough to fit three men. There was nothing but a desk, and a chair, a lamp and a safe. Not even a framed photograph on the desk; Spartan décor for a sterile business office.

Re-entering the main artery of the building, he spied a room at the end of the building. The layout of this place was too small. This had to be where Taylor hid. He passed through the main mourning area; it was littered with scattered chairs. He entered through the jade colored door into a workroom.

Rich swamp wood shavings permeated the air. Coffins sat stacked while various tools for cleaning the blood out of a body and a table sat to the right. A lot of work went on in this cramped space.

The floor was a jagged concrete slab with stains all shades of the rainbow married to the floor. An old crucifix hung above the bloodletting table, Christ's eyes seemed to ache more than normal. The overbearing gloom in this house of eternity was enough to make even him depressed. Breathing heavy behind a stack of four oak coffins, Ed Taylor clutched a rifle he used to carry on his horse.

"Why'd you think retiring to New Orleans would save your sorry ass? You might have the demons 'round this town of whores fooled, not me. I know who you are." The Ghost hollered. Taylor's eyes twitched while his heart ran a marathon in his chest.

The sound of the footfalls of the heavy black boots grew nearer. Taylor took a big swallow.

The Ghost fired a shot into the room, making Snake Eye stain his trousers. The opium was kicking around inside of his skull. He let a shot go into the ceiling, giving his position away.

The Ghost pointed both barrels at the stack.

"Did it feel good? Didya feel immortal? You destroyed my life. For what? Money. The money your sorry hide will pay out when I collect what the state of Texas wants for your head. I ain't even gonna spend the bounty. I'm gonna waste it." He paused to let the flow of information sink in.

Snake Eyes Ed Taylor clicked the hammer into place.

His choices were few. He'd take a blind shot, hoping to nick the son of a bitch.

"How'd you ever think taunting me would scare me?" The Ghost called out.

"Danny Boy's a goner. He's buried up on the hill next to his pappy in Madrid. Pushed his old man in the line of fire. Killed the man that give him life. He broke his father's body, worse he broke his heart."

Taylor remembered the thud of Mattie's body when she hit the floor. It felt so black and white in his memories, like a life ago. Back then he seemed invincible. While the others laughed at the legends of the bounty hunter and welcomed the famed gunfighter to seek them out, he did his best to cover tracks.

Once a brother in red—always a brother in red.

They used to pledge it to one another before a gunfight or a robbery. Taylor took a second to look at his tattoo on his hand and gave it a quick kiss.

Taylor stared at the dull metal of his gun barrel.

He pointed it backward and took a shot in the general direction he figured The Ghost was in. The drugs swirled up his senses. The boom didn't hit The Ghost. The shot was wide to the right. Bits of ceiling and wall fell to the ground. Breathing was the only sound in the room. Taylor yelled over the coffins.

"Ye, I know who you is. Knew you'd come lookin' fer me. You're a killer like the rest of us. Funny thing, your devils don't pay as well." His words were slow, and a lot of thought was laid into them as he fought through the brume of the drugs.

"I tried to turn my life 'round. I regret what I done. You can believe that. I'm an old man. I see the world a bit different these days. I'm fallin' apart.

"It's a shame we had ta meet this way. It's my fault." Taylor lowered his weapon as the depth of his words took a hold of him. He gave up the fight as he spoke.

"I remember when we rode out to Chicago. Selling guns to Yankees settling their neighborhoods. After the war, I guess guns was hard to come by, so we ride up there hauling some major artillery. Folks stared at us like we'd crawled out from the Goddamned funny papers. Seeing them tall buildin's and the people made us feel smaller than ants. We ain't ever seen such a sight. No dust on their boots and no space to roam free. Them people were in one big cage. Some reason bein' up there made me reflect. I recall feelin' mighty small, powerful aimless. I did a lot of mean-hearted things, and while I felt like I was top' a the world, I weren't but shit.

"Maybe the fresh air and space does it to men, makes 'em feel like God ain't at their heels. But, when you see so many folks in one place not flinchin' when you stroll past, but look atacha like you was a novelty in your boots and hat, it was right strange. They got real policemans, not sheriffs who'll dole it out. I thought of you. I thought of what we done, all the things we done. One time we took a man's hands because he owed us a little cash. We coulda shot him. We didn't. We took his fuckin' paws. I held the feller down while the Indian hacked away. We ruined his life."

Taylor genuinely began to sound sadder as he spoke. "I sat there by that lake, listening to the waves crash against the rocks. I just rode damn half across creation for what? To sell some man in a suit some guns. I didn't need the money, I didn't need anything, but this hole in my soul makes me want to do nothing but mean-hearted things. I may be an old fucker now with a busted eer'thing, but I know in my heart I ain't shit. I deserve that bullet."

The Ghost's two pistols both fired at the coffins. Bullets cut through the wood and into Ed Taylor. Both guns went click. The iron balls struck a lung and clean through the left shoulder. The side of the neck poured out like a hog for slaughter.

The Ghost stood over Ed Taylor. His face was hidden under the long brim of his hat.

"Did you think I'd let you give a sermon on how you'd changed?"

Ed Taylor gasped for air as blood filled his lungs. Writhing on the floor, Taylor's blood stained everything it touched. A burnt shade of brown colored the debris on the floor, and the coffins blown to smithereens.

The Ghost scooped up Ed Taylor's shotgun off the ground. He aimed it at Ed Taylor's neck and pulled the trigger.

«‹‹ — ›››

The rains came through that night. Loud claps of thunder shook the wooden buildings to their studs while the lightning lit up the night sky. The Ghost lay in his soft hotel bed. His eyes raced over the intricate details in the ductwork, the wooden trim lining the room. From the way the wood fit together, to the precise lines of paint; it calmed him.

He'd been lucky so far. Many fell victim to the bloodlust in a vendetta. He was no better than any of those men. Two of the seven were face down in the grave. Neither challenged him, save a stab wound. It couldn't last. There was no way it would be this easy. These men were killers, and thieves—they'd never lie down to die with arms open.

The thunder cracked the sky in a loud BANG! He was sure somewhere in town, a babe screamed in fear from the monolithic celestial roar. The natural symphony bellowed outside his window. The chaotic, nurturing rains soothed his inner animal.

All that remained of his childhood were memories; memories were all he had to cling to in such an emotionally bankrupt world. The past let him remember the details, or, at least, pretend to envision the world not filled with blood and cruelty.

It had been many moons since The Ghost knew what family was or meant. They gave one another space and closeness. Theirs was a place a love and trust. A home with a father to seek council, and a mother teaching how to exist in a world filled with crooks and heartbreak.

His brother, the constant companion, and co-conspirator in crimes around the ranch was his rock, his best friend. He was now The Ghost's source of constant pain.

Oh Daniel, how I miss you.

When The Ghost returned home after the war, he learned his mother caught something wicked and passed. Her blood was poison, thus driving a proud, hard woman kicking and screaming into the grave. His father was long dead, and now, the Masterson boys only had one another. And now, Daniel was gone, too.

A father lost to the ravages of hard work in a cruel world, and his mother, dead long before the expiration date due to the biology of faulty genes.

It would be a while before he'd fall asleep. When he did drift off, his family would be in his dreams. It was a beautiful sight to see them all together again.

THE FIXER

Word spread through the New Orleans gutters that Ed Taylor was dead. Apparently, he had pull in the New Orleans underworld. Taylor's fat companion was named Lester Holbrook, a dime store pimp known for running sketchy card games. He'd spread the word to his connections: The Ghost didn't walk: he floated as he hunted them down.

Holbrook blew a long-winded speech about The Ghost to a few key players in the underground circuit in a smoky room off Dauphine Street. Stumping like a politician for pork barrel interests, sweat dripped off the Holbrook's face.

The Ghost was a mythical "killer of killers"—anyone who put such a man down, became a feared legend themselves.

Holbrook's jowls shook, and his meaty fists slammed together in crocodile-teared rage. By playing on people's raw emotions, he could climb the social ladder. Comrades come and go, but money and status could be attained, and this was his chance to rise from the sewers. The price was set: $100 cash money for the head of The Ghost. And in a city like New Orleans, $100 went a long way.

After a day or so of rest, The Ghost appeared from his cocoon in the hotel. Rested, he wanted to thank his new friend,

Simon. He'd buy him a drink before jetting out of town for the next leg of the journey. Down in the bar, bodies spoke under the din of the trumpet buzzing on the street corner. The trumpeter wasn't blasting the patrons with over zealous anthems; he stirred a pot, thick and dark. His brilliant sound added color to the conversational, sticky roux brewing.

Simon's bar was abuzz with living shadows. The crib girls sat on laps, and a few men sat around the bar either embattled in card games or telling war stories over the bottle. Simon, at the far end of the bar, talked to a big boned whore busting out of her cheap corset. The Ghost sat alone, sipping on bourbon.

Simon flirted with the big girl. He'd chat with The Ghost in a minute. He was laying the groundwork for a freebie later. For a while, it was a nice change of pace for The Ghost. The drinks came on the regular and the atmosphere was steady and interesting. This was the way he liked to leave the Crescent City: with a smile on his face. Snake Eyes was dead and he had a few dots he could connect. Maybe try California or Florida next—those seemed like logical places for the reminder of the gang to hide in plain sight.

Two pairs of road-worn, dusty boots walked in the bar. Simon looked up at them; these two were up to no good. He could tell by their dog-faced sneers and boot black crud staining their skin.

They had a score to settle. It was immediate they weren't here for an after work cocktail. Simon froze as he stared at bloodshot eyes scanning the bar. Trouble brewed.

The Ghost faced away from the door, tucked off from a casual glance. The men sought him out, knowing where he sat. The two goons strode toward him with hatred in their hearts.

They stood behind him and looked The Ghost over. He felt the eyes on his back. He felt their labored breaths but didn't move. One of the bodies dropped down beside him while the other stood feet away. The tension was thick and personal.

The Ghost didn't acknowledge the body inches from him. The man sighed and sucked the saliva off his rotten teeth. He set his sun beaten hat on the bar. His filthy fingers slid through his mud and sweat black trusses. The man's greasy hair glistened like tallow from mire. He stunk of cut-rate liquor, wood smoke, and bloodshed. A hard luck bastard with nothing to lose, one of his kind, a real shit kicker. The man's eyes were coral from drink and tears. His face was ashen with grime, and soot.

The man sucked in a great snot from deep within and blew it on the ground where it festered. He used his sleeve as a handkerchief and made a large audible swallow, announcing to The Ghost he wanted to chat.

"Ever seent a man build a gallows?"

"Yes sir, I have," The Ghost replied, still not making eye contact.

"This one time, I done some day labor in a fuck all town out in Missouri. They was fixin' to hang coupla niggers. Can't say I remember why they was getting hanged, but it don't matter none, anyhow. So, I builds 'em a beautiful place to string these coons up. I Made sure it could handle any kinda fightin' or thrashin. When I was all finished, I sat are' and watched 'em the next day. Them black boys had tears in they eyes. Real sad. You know what I did?"

"Can't say I know."

"I laughed my fuckin' ass off."

"There a moral to this story?" The Ghost asked.

"Nope. I just like seein' motherfuckers die."

The Ghost knew this game. The man seated next to him toyed with any emotional lean he could get. He begged for a rise, for attention. Only an animal talks to a stranger with such brazen solidarity. The Ghost wasn't impressed.

"You're lookin' fer me, Ghost," he said.

The Ghost didn't make eye contact but chose to remain focused on his bourbon.

"That a fact? And who might you be?" The Ghost answered aloof.

The man presented a ragged red sash with a seven embroidered on it. He tossed it on top of the bar. A cold shiver surged up The Ghost's spine.

"'At's who the fuck I am." The man's eyes stood out fairy tale white against the dirty layer of crud on his face. His pupils dilated while his teeth looked craggy and jagged. He bubbled with anticipation. This dog wanted to tangle, and bad.

"Put yer fuckin' hands flat on at bar top. Move 'em and ole boy here'll turn yer head ina' a canoe."

The Ghost said nothing. He moved his hands into place.

He hummed. He kept his cool. By not putting on a show, the stranger beside him grew angry. By not playing into his Stone Age advances, The Ghost was in his aggressor's head.

"Well, let's solve this here riddle. I like playin' games. Don't look like a wetback, so you ain't Cortez or Hidalgo. You ain't Indian—that's for sure. I hear he's mighty big, and you're pretty puny. You're white as I am, minus a bath. So, you're either the man they called "The Fixer" or Phineas Alexander and friend, you don't look like you're smart enough to be titled Phineas. Gonna use the power of deduction and go with Mr.

Red "The Fixer" Montague." The Ghost turned his head and met the man's eyes.

"You Goddamned right. That's who the fuck I am. Lookit yew bein' all full of sense." Montague croaked. He tried to peer into The Ghost but what he saw was abhorrent violence, chaos.

"So, Mr. Fixer—what do you fix?" The Ghost asked.

"I ain't fixed nothin' in a spell. 'Ese days, I'm into breakin' much as I can. Call it some sort of vi-o-lent affliction, I reckon. Got nothin' to live for, might as well break the Goddamned world with me. Theory as ya'll smart folks call it—At what I'm runnin' with."

"Sounds complicated. Glad I ain't trapped inside that thick head of yours."

The Ghost knew a little about The Fixer from stories told around the campfire. According to a few boys who'd dealt with him knew The Fixer was a soul feigned for destruction. No will to live, and always ready to die, he knew his existence was worthless and wore it as a badge of honor. He beat the hangman's noose once and left a red scar around the base of his neck for life; thus the mark establishing his obsession with the gallows.

His daddy killed his momma when he was a baby. Daddy walked out of the house, never looked back. The child lay in filth, crying for milk and love for God knows how long. A friend of his momma stopped by their shack at the end of a long dirt road to a baby half alive; tears streaked down his face.

From that day forward, Red hated the world around him. He never bothered with school, never kept a wife and did everything in his power to make his name infamous. His only joy was watching the world wither away with each sin he tallied, and the Bible offered plenty of options. He taunted and abused what most kept sacred. It was an essential bit of the fabric of the man he was.

"I ain't here to be cute with you. Yer a cur and I intend to splatter your guts far as I can see. I'm here to put you down for murderin' my best friend. If yer here to kill him, I knows yer here lookin' fer me. I wanted to come right to yew and tell yew to go fuck yerself. I ain't scared of yew." Montague spat on the ground.

"Well, shit. I got news that'll break your heart."

The Fixer snarled his lip and waited for this bastard in black to piss him off worse. He begged him to give him a reason to cut his belly open right here, right now. A tiny smirk crept across The Ghost's face. He turned and looked at The Fixer.

"Danny Boy's dead as a doornail. Hope that ruins your day since you're so emotional and all."

He fingered the peashooter hidden up his jacket sleeve and since it was a .22 caliber bullet, if he got off a good shot, it would buy him a few seconds to pull out the revolvers and take these boys to town. He needed to be smart with this conversation, set the dominos up and let them fall.

"You k-killt Danny Boy? Yew Goddamn son a whore." He felt Montague's furious breath closer to him than before.

"When I put a bullet between them eyes, I won't feel a lick of shame, either." The Ghost beamed.

"At fact? Yew think yer killin' me? Yew might be big and bad in all them bullshit stories. Yer the one gonna be throwed in the ground, hoss. Personally, yer house weren't no different than anyone else's I didn't give two fucks about you, and still don't."

Montague paused. He sucked the filmy saliva from across the front of his teeth. His choppers looked like abused razor blades left out from a suicide pact.

"Boo," said The Ghost. The Fixer gave a big smile.

"I was the one who put the slug right in the little fucker's head. One shot. BAM! Yew took from me and mine, t'was only fair. I'm bout to skull fuck you jus' the same as I did yer kin."

He blew the smoke away from the imaginary barrel and re-holstered his weapon.

"You're a real piece of shit," the Ghost hissed. His knuckles were bloodless against the wood of the bar top.

"I'm a lot of thangs, mister. I intend to be a gravedigger today."

Simon watched from his end. His whore babbled on. Her enormous, flabby breasts sat atop the bar. He'd seen her dog and pony show a million times. He pretended to pay attention while watching the situation with his new friend escalate.

The rage in The Ghost's eyes burned blue with a severe fire reserved for a funeral pyre. The man standing behind the two at the bar stepped closer and now aimed his piece at The Ghost's noggin. Below the bar, Simon cocked the rifle he kept in case of emergency.

Montague paid Simon no mind. He engaged in a dance to the death. Against his better judgment, Simon knew he shouldn't involve himself in another man's woes, but without knowing much of anything, he knew the two loathsome bastards were no good. The caitiff to the right of The Ghost took extreme pleasure in his role as the agitator, and Simon saw his orchestra of sadism spilling over into full on terrible ultra violence. Simon kept the rifle at the ready, waiting to see how this played out.

Montague spat again, digging the chaw out of his cheek and throwing the putrid brown wad to the floor. The Ghost still said nothing. His mind went over a series of options and what was the best route of attack in such a precarious situation. The smugness of Montague was enough to make him want to kill him with his bare hands. Doing this right meant taking his time and moving with the tide. He let the villain take control.

"Git up. We're goin' fer a walk. I ain't gonna kill you in here. I like this place jus' fine. Don't wanna ruin a good drinkin' hole with the memory of killin' you in it." He paused. "Then again, might make me happy, too." The Ghost tickled the mechanism that'd spring the little peashooter into action. He'd have to spin around, hoping the bullet landed in the sentry before managing to pull his guns. Montague was armed. He knew Montague would blow a hole in his head the moment they were out of the bar.

He had to kill The Ghost outside where conflicting reports could save his skin so he wouldn't get strung up for murder.

The Ghost's legs pushed the barstool to a slide across the wooden floor. His palms next moved flat over the grains of the wood on the bar top. The heat from his skin left small impressions of heat across the surface. For a split millisecond, his eyes met with Simon's.

The Ghost offered a grave rendition of a grin to the sentry with his shaking hands. The sentry was a scrawny kid in a too big, dirty trainman's cap.

The Ghost felt the crushing fear in the furrowed brow of the child. He was no more than sixteen and all nerve.

"Son, why are you tooting a piece for this fuck up? You'll end up dead. I don't wanna hurt you. We ain't got business. Put your barrel down." He thumbed at Montague.

"Keep talkin' dead man," Montague replied.

The Ghost paused on his heels. The two men stood at each side. The scared kid's hands shook wildly. Montague noticed, giving him a quick stink eye. The Ghost took this pause to deconstruct the two of them. The kid would shit his pants. He wasn't fast: he was frightened.

"You're the idiot sister fucker who coulda rolled outta here without me not knowing a thing. I'd of chased you down, but you could have gone anywhere, and you stuck around. You coulda ran oft to Canada and it'd of taken me a lifetime to catch you. You're as dumb as you look."

"Keep talkin' I ain't the one bout to get my brains painted in the mud." The Fixed reminded him.

"Your best friend pointed a gun at me. Didn't work out in his favor," said The Ghost.

A sliver of hatred ignited within Montague. He felt a wonton, dire need to kill The Ghost. Fuck the consequences. Infuriated, Montague took a lunge with his pistol and clapped The Ghost.

The Ghost fell, scraping his face against the copper railing at the bottom of the bar. A thin vein of dark blood trickled out of the right side of his mouth. He lay there for a few seconds while Montague slammed his boot toe into his side. The game was on. Movement erupted from all directions. The stars danced across The Ghost's vision. Montague moved like a man possessed. In this paint swirl of time, everything was in flux. Anger permeated the void. The bullet froze in the air, the voracious moment of finality crept into the mouths of the living, deep tongue kissing the soul.

The kid stumbled forward as the shot from Simon's rifle blew a hole right through him. The body crumpled in a crying heap. Blood splattered the bar top. The kid lay in a ball on the floor, a babbling mess. Montague fired a few off-kilter shots toward Simon in retaliation. The customers fell to the ground, pulling their tables up as shields against stray bullets. Drinks spilled across the dirty wooden floor as Montague's boots scrambled across it as well. One of Montague's bullets struck the fat whore. Blood spattered down her enormous tits. Her eyes rolled back and within seconds, she was gone. No one would avenge her. A few drunkards would remember her name.

Simon ducked behind his bar. Beer glasses and rye whiskey bottles shattered as Montague fired. The Ghost rolled between Montague and the kid, firing a shot from his peashooter into Montague's left thigh. A small pocket of blood exploded as the shock sent his weight buckling down. Montague fired two shots in the body of The Ghost in rapid, un-aimed succession.

One bullet crashed through his belly, sending a white hot pain through his abdomen and up into his teeth. Another shot nicked enough of his neck to bleed. He wouldn't have long before the lights went dim, and he'd be a goner.

The dead hooker slumped in a pile of flesh in front of Simon. He used her sturdy frame as a human shield. Peeking around her, he fired another round out of the barrel of the Sharps. This time he made a direct hit to Montague's back in the kidney territory. Montague squealed with torment.

The Ghost fired off a few shots himself, landing a few killers. Montague fell face first onto the grimy floor. On his way down, he blew off one last shot off, sinking into The Ghost's left shoulder. The lights went out.

The Ghost felt the room fall away. The life flowed out of him like a dazzling crimson river, and the gloaming silence was comforting. A calmness rose. Death embraced him, and it felt right to die.

Off in the distance, down a long hallway, he could make out a clamoring of bodies. Sounds. Screams.

He heard the kid's faint cries for his momma, pleading to the God who shunned him, swearing he'd do right by him, as long as he'd let him see another day. The kid's mouth was a cruel frown. Everything felt distant and hollow as the world circled the drain. The Ghost felt nothing. The kid's cries sounded acres away. With a decent surgeon and a bottle he'd pull through; this was what the doctor ordered to get his act together. Lucky for the kid, the buckshot destroyed his back, and not his front or vital organs.

There was a ripping tone of immediacy to Simon's voice, and as The Ghost felt himself floating, the blood of the world swirled around him. The real ghosts watched as his eyes worked behind the lids while the living world hollered. All of the men he'd killed came to him. Snake Eyes, Montague and Danny Boy's hideous death faces fresh from The Big Fire wafted their scaly tongues over his drifting body. The blood dripped out of him one grain of sand at a time. Soon it would be all over. Everything went black.

«« — »»

Like the winding motion of a music box turned to a full click, The Ghost's eyes flew open days later. It was night. The room he lay in was illuminated with candles. The surroundings were strange; he wasn't in his hotel room or a hospital. Bandages covered his frame. Breathing felt like suicide. Next to his bed sat a precarious young woman.

She leaned over him, her pewter crucifix hanging between her breasts, almost hitting him in the face. Her eyes were a smoky alley cat gray while the fantastic flames of auburn hair bunched up in a schoolgirl knot.

"Well, you ain't dead."

"Appears I ain't." The beautiful figure above grew more into focus.

"Don't try to do too much. You lost a lot of blood. Papa tried real hard to keep you living. Hate to see you bust a stitch." The girl spoke in a sweet tone. Her warmth was overpowering. In the candlelight, her features shined. She was knitting.

"W-who're you?" he whispered. As he tried to move any part of his body, he was met with excruciating agony.

"Annabelle Simon. My daddy's got an odd love for you, mister. We've been watching you for days now. You took a few shots in your last gunfight that'd leave a lesser man in the grave. How in all hell daddy saved you is beyond me. You're damned lucky to be alive. He took those bullets out of you himself."

Simon. His new friend saved him from an early grave.

"Be sure to tell him thanks."

"I was you, I'd find a moment to thank your creator, but by the looks of you, I can tell you have not had a conversation with God in a long time."

"Store's been closed."

He was enthralled by her kindness. She tapped his hand laying on his chest like a corpse in a casket.

"Rest up, feller. I'll tell daddy about you in the morning. He pops in to check on you throughout the day. He'll be pleased as punch you opened your eyes. That'll take his stressin' way down. Get some sleep. You ain't no good to the world or us if you're nothing' but half alive."

The Ghost tried to talk, but Annabelle laid a finger across his lips.

"Get on, sleep."

Feeling an immense sense of comfort he slipped into what seemed like sleep that regenerated his soul.

When his eyes opened next, the breeze danced across his skin from the open window across from his bed. The Ghost smelled the repulsive smell of shit being cleaned up in the streets and heard a brass band stomping a Dixieland tune in a courtyard.

His body ached, but at least, he could sit up.

The room was empty and quiet. His clothes lay out on a chair. He noticed his revolvers. His boots shined. His jacket and pants didn't look like they'd been shot up or covered in blood—maybe Annabelle mended them? He tried to rise. Pain overtook once again.

His shoulder was in a half sling. He saw through a black eye and spoke through a busted bottom lip. He'd done a splendid job at messing himself up this time. Breathing was cumbersome and labored. He wanted so bad to get up.

He tried again. His feet swung over the side of the bed, and through astounding, obscene agony, he sat up. He looked out of the window to the streets below. Charters Street brimmed with life as New Orleans does. The sun felt wonderful tickling his face. He closed his eyes for a second and took in the pleasure of being alive while he had this moment to himself. He was thankful. Someone looked out for him. Even though he knew next to nothing about the man, or why he'd stuck his neck out for him—

"Mighty fine day out there in the world today." Simon said from the doorway. His eyes were tired.

Naked from the waist up save his suspenders, he took a seat in the chair next to the bed. He lit a pipe and instantly, the saccharine scent of cherry tobacco filled the room. The Ghost moved toward the back. Nudging back amongst the pillows, he faced Simon.

"You saved my ass."

"Just doin' what I figured was right."

The Ghost felt terrible. The poison of healing gripped his body and made his stomach churn. Getting out the words was taxing, but important.

Simon took a long, contemplative pull off his pipe. The cherry-scented smoke rolled around in his mouth for a second before releasing it.

"When I look at yew, I don't see a monster. I see a man standin' by his morals."

Simon continued after pulling a long drag on his pipe.

"Losin' yer family like that, that shit haunts me. I lose sleep over a hair being misplaced on my daughter's head. A man willin' to die for his family, I respect the heart it takes te stare death in the face. I'd ride through the war without a horse for my Annabelle. Seein' yew get gunned down jus' weren't gonna happen so long as I could help it."

The Ghost held out his hand. Simon gripped it. They were brothers deep as the ocean, bonded by a crimson constitution. For the next few hours, The Ghost spilled his guts.

Regaling the stories from his years on the trails and the hard life he'd led thus far; he told him about sharp shooting for the union. To him, it was a mess, and that obtrusive, skeletal mess mutated him. He waxed poetic to Simon, inch by detailed inch of his land, the place where his parents and brother rested.

"I've one question." Simon looked at him sharply. "Why you call yerself The Ghost? Dramatic, ain't it?" The Ghost looked over at this black clothes, black boots, and steel black gun. The blade of his knife was a dull black color.

"After the war, I was a confused man. We kept the country together; we killed our own, and for fuckin' what? Humanity's fucking awful. This world is a Goddamned dog bowl of vermin and slobber.

"I stripped myself of all possessions. I became an idea, not a man. When the war was over, they stuck us out there slaughtering and scalping Mexicans and Indians. It was then that I knew we were a pale-faced, evil people living in a society built on bullshit; we're the people who've already stolen land and we're murdering more folks so we could steal more."

Simon's eyes sailed far away, watching the tops of his feet rocking side to side. He listened, lost in his war-torn nightmares.

The Ghost continued: "Towns burned because American crooks wanted it all. In their wake, they left children face up, and full of bullets. I ain't God-fearing; I got no religion." He drifted into a distant place.

"I call myself The Ghost 'cause I walk in the darkness of the heart, I do what many men won't."

Simon stood at the window. His hands rubbed the grains of the wood. The silence laid enough track between them. Simon looked out below into the world of New Orleans. French drunks argued with one another while Americans crept up behind, stealing their effects. No one would persecute the Americans.

New Orleans scared Simon, but he'd made his money here. There was nothing left for him in Kansas. This was home. He never knew how he'd talked himself into staying here after The Battle for this city. After Simon had drifted along in a maudlin trance of being a soldier, he found this town, this chaotic, ruinous place.

"That's mighty fine reason, friend. Can't blame yew for not understanding this world. Was out there in them battles, too. I know what it feels like to be lost in a sea of hatred and violence. The truth is, I saved ye because I seen myself in you. I'm a man who lost his world and didn't understand it so. My bride Victoria died when Belle was born. It broke me." Without her pulling me outta the darkness, I'd be a dead man. I managed to beat my demons and survive a war. I earned some scars, but I don't like for seein' good men suffer same as me."

Simon moved to the doorframe. He looked his friend over, offering a weak, sincere grin, and went out.

The Ghost lie still, his wounds ached.

The Ghost drifted off into a vacuous sleep where the world stopped. In his dreams, he sat on a porch strumming a beaten down guitar. Songs bled from his fast moving hands, giving a musical sermon to the damned souls.

He played as the world spiraled into the abyss.
Annabelle was there in a short summer dress, with a
bow in her hair. Her feet kicked, while her eyes
burned bright.

Sinner, please don't let this harvest pass
Sinner, please don't let this harvest pass

Sinner, please don't let this harvest pass
And die and lose your soul at last.

The Ghost sang loud. As the words jumped from his
throat, the world shifted. The wind picked up and
howled. Annabelle never moved, her feet kicked at the
winds of the grim reapers cloaked arm, vacating the
earth of its souls. She stayed next to him, glued by the
voracity of pleasure in the creeping death of
humanity. The inky black sky coalesced into a
multiplicity of wild colors. A vicious crimson hue
undulated into a dark, royal blue and a farmhouse
green, spiraling inward creating a vortex surreal to
anyone unlucky enough to witness the spectacular
sight of the known realm dying. The Ghost played on.
The show in the sky kept twisting and turning into a
chaotic, terrible gateway, opening up to Gods will
and the devil's due. Both sides came to collect the
hearts and minds of their flock. The corvids squawked
and hollered in the trees above. The atmosphere
floated away.

I my Redeemer lives
I my Redeemer lives
I my Redeemer lives
Sinner, please don't let this harvest pass
Sinner, O see the cruel tree
Sinner, O see the cruel tree
Sinner, O see the cruel tree
Where Christ died for you and me

My God is a mighty man of war
My God is a mighty man of war
My God is a mighty man of war
Sinner, please don't let this harvest pass

The scarecrows out in the fields moved their bodies,
swaying with the breeze of finality. Their straw
fingers danced through the cutting winds, their
threaded faces moaning as the strings giving their
expressions popped on stitch at a time. The earth
shook with a violent, daring ferocity.

«« — »»

A soft hand touched his cheek, and it was over. The Ghost opened his eyes, and the world was not ending, he was back in bed. Annabelle sat beside him. Dinner. Relief washed over him as an overwhelming sense of comfort was present.

"Bad dream?"

"Nah. Dancing babies smoking cigars. It was cute. Shoulda been there."

"Take your word for it."

"What took you so long to come see me today?" he asked.

"Girl's got chores, you know. I made dinner. This's yours. You're still pretty poor off. So I made gumbo. Hope you like it."

"Bet my hat it tastes like heaven. Set down for a spell."

"Can't. Need to feed daddy. He wanted you fed first. Rest up and I'll check in on you after a while." She was redder than a spring plum. A small fire burned between them.

He wished he could take one deep swallow of her scent and hold it in his lungs. After finishing his meal, he contemplated his life for a while. Who he was he? What he needed to do, and where the sun directed him remained the constants.

When he woke next, he continued analyzing his road traveled thus far. He looked at his revolver and repeated the inscription again and again:

Behold the Pale Horse—Behold the Pale Horse—Behold the Pale Horse—he couldn't sell this short. He'd be damned if he didn't see it through.

«« — »»

Weeks passed and he felt his strength returning in spades. He walked around the house, almost at full health. He helped Simon around the bar and did what he could around the house to not feel like a freeloader. The Ghost took his time reading some of the books Annabelle kept around the house. He'd considered the perspective of worlds he only imagined, and as he read, his mission to finish what he started became clearer by the day. This vacation from his life felt great, but as his brother's bones collected dust, he wasn't in the mix, avenging the destruction of his bloodline.

It was hard not falling in love with this life; he'd lean in on Annabelle as she cooked, not long before she'd shoo him away. Her grace was staggering.

She'd holler at him for being up and chase him back into bed. Having her around was comforting; Annabelle brought ease into his life. Their talks grew longer, and before long, he'd hobble down to the French Market to buy groceries with her.

He couldn't afford much weight, but he worked real hard to carry the bread or carrots. Seeing Annabelle smile at his trials of regaining his sense of self made him work harder.

When he stopped down to the bar for an occasional whiskey, patrons offered him a round or two, hearing the legend of the man who'd survived such a brutal ordeal and even better, killing two badmen in the process. He enjoyed the numbing effects of the bottles of whiskey as his body healed. He and Simon became genuine friends, having heart to heart talks almost daily, between squeezing in as much flirting with Annabelle as her sense of conduct allowed.

When he felt good enough not to use a cane to hobble around with any longer, he wrapped his shoulder and stomach himself. The stitches would be able to be taken out soon. He'd done it before. His neck was healed. Despite the ache in his heart, he had to leave them. When he rose in the mornings, his first thought wasn't killing. Instead, it was the sweet smell of Simon's only daughter.

«« — »»

He slipped out of the house without saying a word. Neither Simon nor Annabelle heard a peep as he made his way out. The sun wasn't up yet. New Orleans slept under a blanket of drunken stars, the crashing waves of the Mississippi lulling them to sleep. A rolling fog added ease to his escape. The Ghost had risen. In his place was a stack of money, and a note:

Dear Brother Simon & dearest Annabelle,

You knew this is how'd I skip out. Ain't nothing personal.

I need to finish my business. It's my oath. I can't rest till those bastards are all in holes or lying in a burning heap.

I thank you for the kindness you both showed me. I owe you my life.

I'd dead as dirt if it wasn't for your love and kindness. I'll never forget it for the rest of my days.

By saying as much, I am offering my land as a gift. It's the Masterson family land. Ain't none finer. Please, if you want to get out of New Orleans, follow the map I've enclosed. I've already sent a letter to a friend letting him know of my plans. The land is yours if you care to take it.

But this ain't a free ride. If you take this land, take it knowing for the rest of your days you'll be working in pristine wilderness with blue streams and sunshine. You'll be starting from scratch. The cabins are all gone.

Simon, take the land knowing when I ride home, I'll be doing it with the intent of forming a partnership. I wanna get in business: the business of building a fantastic life for you, Annabelle, and me—If you'll allow her to marry me.

I'll see you both in my dreams. When I ride upon the ridge overlooking the ranch, I hope to see two horses, and I'll know it's my turn to settle down like my family before me.

Ghost.

《《《 — 》》》

The fog was knee high and soupy thick. The city of New Orleans, the living graveyard. Jackson Square's haunted spires beckoned to God despite the surrounding haze. His boots clicked along the manicured slate on his way to get his horse. It'd been a minute since he'd rode her; he missed the feeling of riding against the wind toward destiny. He needed to get out of The Crescent City.

If Simon or Annabelle caught him, they'd demand he wasn't ready. His health wasn't their problem any longer. They'd all settle up on at the ranch if they chose to take him up on the offer. Till then, his heart was closed for business.

CORTEZ

He rode toward a local legend for all bad men. A Mexican whorehouse where inhibitions went to die, it had some fancy bullshit name in Spanish, but all who paid a visit knew it by its nickname: The Bucket of Blood.

Two of the men on his list happened to be in New Orleans. It was fool's thinking the rest would be close by. The Ghost was lucky to get two for the price of one, save the bullets that laid out him for a spell.

The Bucket was a safe bet. Someone around the acrid shit hole had information for sale. All it took was money. Those dogs would sell out their own mothers. It would take days riding through the Comanche territory, but it was worth it. Reaching Chalky, she snorted, shaking her head. The Ghost gripped her long skull to his chest in a tight embrace. She danced with joy. The Ghost furnished an apple and rubbed his hands down the snout of his closest companion. Tossing his saddle and bags over his beast, it felt good to sitting atop a horse once again. He'd spent way too much time on his own feet.

The Bucket of Blood sat out in Laredo where America ended, and Mexico began. His luck in the Bucket wasn't what one would call exceptional, but it was a useful evil. On his last visit, an old nemesis tried to slice off his ear.

Bodies were drug out of the Bucket and thrown into the lake behind the building at least twice a day.

The Ghost and Chalky logged a few good miles on their first day. The towering pines of East Texas died off as the rising hills offered breathtaking views into a vicious, serene, and demanding landscape. The hard stars glowed intense and bright, slashing through the evening with their incandescence. They twinkled for him, promising the future if he could take it. Off in the distance, the coyotes howled at the slate colored face of a daring moon.

«« — »»

The scenery birthed expanse. Cedar and pine gave way to acres of mesquite. Green life fell in number as the dirt underfoot grew sepia and rocky. The brush rolled along with nothing, or no one to stop its path.

Rocky crags met the hooves of Chalky. A dry dust covered all it touched. The rocky red brick mesas, and through the Rio Grande Valley's desert grasslands broke countless cowboys. Flecks of shattered wagon trains spread throughout the area from the Californian gold rush a few years ago. The Tamaulipan Mezquital was a heartless monster. It took pleasure in claiming souls.

Now and again, he'd cross a small area featuring a grave or two with a scrawled name on it, yet another dead from the perilous journey traveling coast to coast.

He inched closer to Del Rio, a fragment of a town near the San Felipe. He could get supplies, perhaps a bite to eat if anything was open by the time he'd reached the town's limits.

The salmon-colored sun dipped lower as the day ached on. The twisting paintbrush of the Gods of the air twined their divine hands through the elements, creating a slick portrait of majestic colors.

The unmistakable scent of mesquite; the land was without many trees, the ones it did have expelled with fragrance. The rains came, and the unforgettable scent of the wet creosote and damp sand whistled through the atmosphere.

He'd made it to Del Rio as the sun fell asleep behind the violet western clouds. Chalky was exhausted, and nearly dead. The Ghost's wounds throbbed.

Makeshift hovels and mud-walled bungalows littered the tiny Mexican town of Del Rio, Texas. Chickens ran wild through the loam streets. Chalky clopped through the dust and clay. A few folks stood by on porches, looking out at the man in black riding past. Looking down at their brown hue, the utter whiteness of the man was alien for this country. No one paid him any mind, but all knew he was there.

He found a room for the night in a tiny ramshackle affair. It wasn't the best of places he'd slept, but it wasn't the worst either. His room was out back, past where the family kept their goats.

The fleshy woman in charge of the building smelled of tobacco smoke and rotten fish. Walking through the town, the sounds of distant mariachi music danced out of one of the decaying adobe buildings. A few drunkards sat with shining, stupid faces, slugging bottles of clear drink. He heard their catcalls to the girls selling the goods, smiling over the railing above. They waited for the drunks to get pissed up enough to make a few bucks. The Ghost saw their sparkling eyes refract light. He found a small shack with a sign lit up by candlelight and took a seat at the bar. The bartender motioned to the wooden menu.

It listed three options in crude scrawl:

–Cervasa
–Wiskee
–Mezcal

The Ghost pointed at beer. The bartender poured him a tall one. It was home brewed, tasting like warm horse spit.

The bartender's face was an ugly patchwork of cuts and scars with crooked, yellow teeth; they looked like a broken accordion.

In broken English, the barkeep explained to The Ghost what was available tonight: Cabrito. They slaughtered a goat earlier. The Ghost ordered and waited. While he sipped on his beer, a card game went on in the corner. The men playing took slugs out of a clay bottle of mezcal while berating one another, and accusing the other players of cheating. His food arrived. Fried chunks of goat meat, tortillas, and paste that were once refried beans.

After a long day riding, he attacked the food. He slid the remaining tortilla through what was left of the pile of beans on his plate. The meal tasted like heaven.

The flesh of the goat sustained him, recharging his system. The card game grew unruly with each passing hand. At least once, one of the drunkards skinned a pistol. The Ghost was surprised no one squeezed the trigger. A sense of foreboding lingered. Washing his meal down with slow sips of beer, The Ghost felt a formidable body stroll into the little tavern.

The presence stood behind him. He kept his eyes down and looked at the scraps of his dinner. He slid his hands down toward his gun.

"Don't even bother you ragged son of a bitch."

The voice was familiar, beyond the grave. Rusty? Could it be? There was no way. Not in this little shit squirt of a town. The Ghost moved on his heels slow, ready for anything. Turning around, there he was, a mirage. Hands on his hips and smiling wide as Texas. Rusty. The Ghost couldn't believe it. The two men embraced in the way old friends could.

"As I live and breath," said The Ghost.

Rusty smiled at his friend, tipping the brim of his hat.

"Yours truly."

"How in the hell?"

"I saw that mangy ass horse of yours sitting at that pile of shit they call a motel. Ain't nobody round' here got a big ole' slick looking black beast. I know one scoundrel with a horse like that. Didn't take much work, so I hunted you down."

"Guess I stick out a little 'round here."

"A little? Shit, son these here Mexicans think Satan hisself is in town. Lookin' at you, they prolly got shit in their breeches. Ain't nobody even think about stealing that horse off you."

Rusty took him under his wing after the war. The Ghost was green and a poor excuse for a bounty hunter. Rusty changed that. He showed The Ghost how to collect the bounty the right way.

Plopping down next to The Ghost, Rusty beamed, taking hold of his friend's black hat. He looked over the sweat stains on the inside, running his thumb along the material.

"What's the story with these fuckers? They're getting plenty loud." Rusty thumbed back at the card game.

"I ain't got the best Spanish, but someone figures another's been cheating. Don't consider myself a swami, but one of these fellers is gonna lose his jaw tonight," The Ghost said, looking over his shoulder.

"The way they're going at that mezcal, I don't doubt it."

The Ghost took a swig of his beer, then wiped the froth from his facial hair.

"'Erry damn time I see you, you get more miserable. Can't you find a thing to wear that doesn't look like you're off to bury your wife? Damn, son. Cheer up for once in your life," Rusty laughed.

"Guess blue just ain't my color."

"Guess not. One can't forget you're "The Ghost"—a living demon or whatever it is the fuck you got people believin' about you. I hear some feller bring you up when tradin' war stories they act like you're a fucking fable. I laugh every Goddamned time."

The Ghost ordered two more drinks from the barkeep. The glasses looked like they'd been washed in the dirt. Rusty swallowed his beer quick.

"What the hell are you doing in this little shithole?" Rusty asked, before motioning to the bartender for a mezcal. "I didn't think I'd ever run into you in all places, these days, especially Goddamned Del Rio. This ain't your route."

"Special delivery. Headed to The Bucket."

Rusty grabbed one of the candles sitting in front of him and pulled it close, lighting his smoke.

"What low down, filthy piece of dog shit you looking for?"

As The Ghost finished with his story, the card table flipped. The dealer and one of the men began slugging one another with harsh blows. Spit and blood stained the money scattered all over the filthy clay floor. The bar watched as fists flew and soon, the two men rolled around on the ground, trying to get the upper hand on one another in between their hollers. As the violence kept its own timbre, the rest of the fellows involved in the card game, picked up whatever cash they could off the floor and slid out of the door.

The Ghost and Rusty looked at one another and began to laugh. No matter where they were together, things always got strange.

"Anyhow, I live here these days. Got me a Mexican woman named Luz I met in my wayfaring travels. I caught a bullet in the ass. Got infected as shit, just about died out in a gulch. Laying there, sweating through an infected ass bullet, that's when I hung up my revolvers. I took up in her hometown and said fuck it." The bartender left the bottle of mezcal in front of them to pour their drinks.

After a few more drinks, a light flicked on in Rusty's head. "I remember them fellers in the red. Their poster hung in the trading post forever. So, not too long ago, a medicine show rolled through town. A mid-sized production, the whole town went to look it over. Guess who's a part of it? Your big Indian they call The Warchief, and the little guy with the black mustache and wet lookin hair. The Indian was a fuckin' monster. Cocksucker's a big motherfucker; the other asshole looks like a wet rat. They weren't foolin' me. Couldn't have been anyone else. I ain't saying it was maybe them: I'm saying it was them. Hunnert percent."

It was good to talk shop with one who'd been there. Rusty understood how he felt. Rusty knew what it was like to be a lone wolf riding for days without so much as uttering a word to a human.

Rusty looked at his pocket watch and slid his feet out. He looked onto The Ghost like a father does to his son.

"I'm old. I've gotta get back my little woman. I miss the long nights and the smell of gunpowder and horseshit. That bein' said I need my home life. Life's too short to be out there trying to right the wrongs of the world. When this is through, I'd bet my ass your sweetheart is waitin' on you with her daddy in tow. You're a good man, Spooky."

He chuckled again.

"Thanks for the faith in me."

"Ain't no faith to it."

"You didn't think I was a punk?"

"Oh, you're still a fuckin' punk."

《《 — 》》

When he slid into bed, he remembered the last time he'd spent with Rusty. Before tonight, it was out in Juarez. Rusty was on the hunt. A man named Telvin Errispon from the Dakotas. Errisponhad a C-Note on his head in relation to slaughtering a band of Italian immigrants from the east heading to the Oregon country—his bounty was a hot ticket.

Dago's from the neighborhood didn't take to the murder of their kin and put together a nice sum on the head of the one-toothed cowpoke.

The Ghost was in Juarez on his own business. He'd received a lead on his hunt for a bank robbing, serial killing band of rouge Apaches fleeing to Central America. He heard from multiple sources they were taking up around the outskirts town. When he and Rusty crossed paths in a saloon at random, it was happiness again. Rusty eyed him, giving a few playful jabs to the ribs. The Ghost agreed to give Rusty back up, seeing as Rusty's man was drunk across the bar with his posse. One against three wasn't great odds, even for the old workhorse.

After Errispon had looked good and impaired, they made their move. Swooping around each side, they pulled their guns. The bandits paused; the two bounty hunters demanded they get on the floor—if they didn't want to be filled with lead. Errispon had no intention of getting strung up.

"You after me?" Errispon asked.

"Betcher ass. You can either rot in a jail cell, or I'm blowin' your brains across this bar. Your call." Rusty answered.

"Neither. I ain't doing shit with the likes of you two. Move along or I'm fixing to put a hurting on you's."

The Ghost raised his revolver higher, leveled at Errispon's face. Errispon looked him over, and when he smiled his rotten black teeth shined.

"Shoulda considered your actions before you killed those people. Anyone who can kill a child and steal his scalp ain't no good." Rusty said with venom in his voice, upset by the killing of children.

"Cashing in scalps was good money. Shame that there wagon train had a buncha black and brown hair. Had they been blonds, they'd be alive to tell the tale," Errispon answered.

Errispon skinned his revolver. He fired. Hanging lamps shattered, as his shots were crooked; the drink sent him off balance. His toadies fired. Rusty and The Ghost dove to opposite sides of the room, Rusty using a card table for shelter while The Ghost hid around the corner of the bar. The rest of the bar took cover.

The bartender sat with his back to the bar with a shotgun clutched to his chest. He'd be ready to pop off on any desperado prepared to grab out of his till.

The Ghost and Rusty emptied their weapons; one of the two who stood with Errispon was a goner. Bullets pierced the air, destroying paintings, and splinter the wooden walls. Rusty landed a sinking shot into Errispon's man's head. In the brief moment of shock, Errispon's eyes left his targeted area and looked down toward his two fallen friends. In the second of doubt, The Ghost took his shot. The ball exploded as the gunpowder created the spark, sending the iron screaming through the chamber of his revolver and into Errispon's throat. Within moments, the dark blood dripping from the side of his mouth puddled next to his body.

It was finished. The Ghost took a bullet to the thigh and Rusty, a slug right in the hand. Their bodies were sweaty and covered in a rainbow of offending odors and liquids. Rusty and The Ghost looked one another over. Each chuckled through his pain. Even when working together, chaos reigned supreme.

The Ghost remained in bed for a day or two following the shooting episode. He'd recover in Juarez, and catch the Apache trail when he was able. If Juarez did something right, it was cheap whiskey and caramel whores who'd turn any Christian into a frothing, reptilian sub-human. With industry such as this, there were worse places to recover.

One morning, a package waited for him at the front desk of his hotel. Ripping the brown paper off, it was a simple black wooden box. When he opened the lid, his heart stopped.

Placed inside was a small note reading: Thank You.

Underneath was a black revolver with an inscribed barrel and an ivory crucifix on the handle.

A widowmaker with *Behold The Pale Horse* inscribed along the barrel.

The very same gun sat in its holster at the edge of the makeshift bed. It was his most prized possession.

«« — »»

He set out toward the Davis Mountains. He'd bought a few provisions and planned to tough it out. The Ghost's mind carried him from the solipsistic heat to thinking of the radiance of Annabelle, the beacon of light. He rode long and hard, and when he reached the base of the mountain he made camp in one of the valleys near burnt umber mesas. Chalky slept in the darkness beyond his fire while he let the universe take his mind wherever it deemed so.

By midday, he'd reached Laredo. The Bucket of Blood was far on the outskirts of town and set on the banks of the Rio Grande. He and Chalky ambled through the toffee colored streets. Watching the store clerks beckon shoppers for their wares, while the coffin maker hammered away at some poor bastard's eternal prison. Since the day it was founded, a sense of foreboding hung over the town of Laredo, Texas. Gloomy clouds brewed above, and they lurched further into the west, casting a sense of vulgarity and doubt over the skulls of passing thieves and drunks looking for mayhem. He found a room in a rooming house dedicated to the comings and goings of the underbelly of society.

The rains fell in blankets outside his window. Even though West Texas was an arid, dry land, when it rained the Gods cleaned out the filth clogging the town. The Ghost fell asleep surrounded by phantoms of the past.

The late afternoon sun was fierce and without repast in afflicting maximum torment unto anyone with exposed flesh.

The Ghost stepped out of the sunlight and into the wanton darkness of the Bucket of Blood. His fingers twitched at the ready while his eyes scanned the scene. The rule in this bar was your money belongs to us. Buy our drink, fuck our whores, throw your dice, but we get a cut. The bartender stood at the ready with arms crossed. His scarred face was a perpetual scowl. A long skinning knife nuzzled his enormous belly, tucked in his belt.

The bartender's tattooed knuckles didn't give off a friendly neighbor next-door vibe. The first commandment of The Bucket of Blood: buy a drink.

The drink was the entrance fee to the circus. Before The Ghost could wrap his head around the carnival of events around him, he paid the man for a beer and a shot of whiskey. He paid in a small bill because he knew he wasn't getting change back.

He slammed the shot. Time to settle into the crowd of thieves, killers, and liars. Eyes watched him. Men shot billiards off in a corner while piles of money sat on the sides.

Card games went on while the knives and guns sat next to beer and money.

A piano player battered out a rousing trail tune while crowds of drunkards linked arm and arm shouted and sang. Their mugs of beer spilled to the sodden floor below. Vampires sat in the darkened corners deep in conversation with one another, brokering nefarious dealings. Wolves in men's clothing chased the plentiful buxom, half-naked Latinas while others paid for their services off in the shadows. The Ghost surveyed the room; he passed a booth where a female form faced the midsection of her momentary employer. The man's face was locked in ecstasy while she worked her magic.

The air stunk with sweat. After a short walk around the long bar, he settled at the far end of the room, waiting for a familiar face. He sipped the beer from his feculent mug, pondering the amount of dead men's lips that have touched the glass.

The man being serviced returned to the living world as the woman between his legs pulled her lips off him. His long, greasy hair hung in his face and over his flushed cheeks. Buttoning up, he rose and shook off the poison that left his body. His girl took notice as The Ghost watched them. She gave him a toothless smile.

After an hour of waiting, his meal ticket walked in. A small, frail fellow with oversized clothes and nervous Chihuahua eyes. He drifted amongst the scoundrels, and no one paid him any mind. He was invisible save the baggy, tattered shirt hanging like bad aura off his skeletal frame. His face was mousey, and his hair was a tangled mess of grime. He took a large, two-handed chug from the mug of beer and let out a burp. His beady eyes looked around like a frightened pest in the kitchen on the hunt for scraps. The Ghost crept up behind him, and as he took a second drink, he spoke.

"Been a spell, Effron."

The small man lowered his mug and sighed after swallowing.

"Shit. I ain't seen you in at least five years?"

"Making a consideration for particular kinds of shitbirds."

"I'm outta the information business. I'm a simple ranch hand dealing in opportunities here and there. Don't know anyone or anything. I'm speek and spann." Effron said.

"Come set down with me. You'll want to hear what I got to tell you. You'd be stupid not to." The Ghost returned to his table with Effron following.

"Effron, we always been straight with one another. Drop the song and dance that you ain't available to work for me, cause we both know for a fuckin' fact that's bullshit." Effron started to speak, but The Ghost continued. "I need the low-down on some folks, nothing that'll get your neck on the chopping block. You'll make yourself a nice pile of money. Don't have me waste my time."

In The Ghost's hand appeared a handful of bills, and fast like a magician, it was out of sight so no eyeballs from around the room would be aware of how much currency he held. Effron's tight lips faded once he saw the amount to which he could ward off working in the fields for a few weeks. He was interested.

"I'm hearing you."

"Good. Need to know where The Red Seven are. Already killed three of 'em."

"The Red Seven. Ain't heard that name in a long while, cabron. Ain't none of them come through here in año."

"Best put your ear to the ground and see what you can shake up. I need to know where they're at. Don't take no for an answer. I ain't in the mood to be disappointed."

Effron looked around the room, but never settling on anyone's face.

"Asking around for a gang that ain't rode through in a while could get people que habla.' I don't want my culo in a sling cause you got a vendetta."

The Ghost took a long drink from his mug and wiped the foam away from his top lip.

"Cut the bullshit. You been a liar and a feeb since knee high to a grasshopper. You lie your way through life. I'll lay a stack of bills in your hand when you get me what I need to know. Your money will make either a whore happy or your bankroll fat considering the little amount of work you'd be doing."

"How much?" Effron asked.

"Enough."

"Gimmie dos dias. Can't promise the moon. I ain't got much to go on if they ain't been in town. No gossip and nobody workin' with them makes it duro."

"Well, that's what I'm payin' you for."

"Which ones you need?"

"My rogue gallery consists of Danny Boy, The Fixer, Snake Eyes."

The Ghost pointed at the wanted poster. Effron studied the names and the X's slashed across the faces of the dead men.

"Why you killin' these hombres?"

"Revenge."

«« — »»

When the knock came to the door, The Ghost rose off the shanty bed upon which he'd been sitting. With his revolver drawn, he moved toward the door. He heard someone breathing through their mouth, and shuffling their feet.

"Who is it?"

"You know damn well who it is. Lemme in."

The Ghost opened the door and swung past it hard with the revolver pointed hard at the air. No one was there aside from Effron. He sighed in relief.

"Put that fuckin' thing down. You not trust me?"

"It ain't you I don't trust, it's the rest of this town I ain't wild about."

"Relax, Cabrone. Nadie sabe que estás aquí To a lot of these young bucks, you're a historia, not even a real persona." The Ghost pondered this. It'd been a while since he'd been in Laredo, and even more since he'd done anything out there in the mix.

They sat at the table at the center of the room. The Ghost pulled out a bottle and poured two drinks. After taking a swallow of the liquid in his glass, he focused his eyes on Effron. His notebook sat close by.

"So, whatcha got?" He asked, ready to get started.

"I got news to sink your teeth in. Your medicine show is called Magic Medicine & Treyebal Speerits by Dr. Axelrod. Your Indio tiron does a lot of business on the sly. Can't say I've heard un sonido. They jumped on the Goodnight Loving headed out to Colorado country. They have been saving almas and selling crap to the local idiotas begging to be reborn, and to see the sick rise from their chinga deathbeds." Effron made a ghoulish wailing sound like a cheap dime store attraction to add temporary effect before continuing. "Mr. Phineas is the master bullshitter. My people tellin' me your Indio is a scary fucker. Word around the campfire says he ripped a man's heart right out of his chest once on the battlefield. Sure it's mierda, but my feller tells me he's frightening."

The Ghost wrote in his notebook. He took another swallow of his drink. Effron's sat untouched.

"The others? Hidalgo and Cortez? You get anything on 'em?"

"Ain't got much. I can say they're back home in New Mex. Cortez runs putas out in Los Alamos or Las Cruces. One of 'em. Guess they call the joint Esmeralda's or some shit. I dunno if that's legit but's it's a good place to start. Got real cute Mexican chicas out there. Cold beer."

The Ghost pulled out Effron's fee with a little extra and slapped the wad in his hand. Effron took the contents of the glass to his lips and swallowed.

The Ghost formulated a plan. He was headed to New Mexico. It was time to see a pair of brothers.

«« — »»

A dark sky boiled and brewed overhead. He was deep into Comanche territory, so The Ghost was on high alert. If they even sniffed at his scent, they'd want his eyeballs on a necklace. A light rain drenched the world for miles. He was soaked, but onward they rode.

The Ghost came to the remains of a burned out little town. He saw from a short distance it looked quiet, and so far on this trip, he'd been lucky to find himself in decent company and with a bed for the evening. The closer he crept toward the scene, it was clear this wouldn't be the case. Nothing within the four clay walls of this nameless town lived.

A slaughter. The adobes were shells of their former selves and the remains of the Mexicans who once prospered here were left to rot in the elements.

The church in the central square looked as if Mammon

himself crawled up from the bubbling flames of hell and declared war upon The House of God.

Its carefully carved cross atop the spire was broken, and one of the arms was hanging while a raven sat atop acting as the caretaker to the church, cawing at the intruder disturbing this place of the dead.

The doors were blown out and what looked like women and children lie vanquished and left for the scavengers. Whatever hit these people couldn't have been too long ago as the permeating smell of blood pugilistically throttled the atmosphere and seeped in the walls and soaked into the grains of wood.

Blue-black hair lie in tangled webs of muck, dirt and blood as the whipping winds slashed through town and grain by grain, the earth took claim to all of her children.

The world was a confusing, and an ultimately disturbing place he was losing touch with: one mile and one terrible sight at a time.

The sun grew dissonant and the air cool, he'd have to find a safe place to lie for the evening, nowhere near this collection of sadness. Anyone who spent any amount of time in such a ruinous, terrible place would feel their heartbreak, and they too would be the riding dead if they didn't opt out and join the haunts surrounding. These scenes of blood red sadness robbed him of the last bits of humanity left within.

«« — »»

When he cuddled up next to the fire, and he closed his eyes and took a few long, deep breaths. The Ghost hoped against nightmares.

Cortez and Hidalgo would sleep naked as jaybirds in beds with a whore or two, their bellies full of greasy meat and powerful booze. They'd pull long slugs out of bottles of tequila, and go on living for the short time they'd been granted serenity in breathing. The Ghost came for their heads.

Men sat in confessionals while others sat ashamed with a pistol in their mouths. The mariachi bands played on while the low rent whores banged away, a dollar at a time. Hard workers and crooks alike were taming the wild country and its wilder natives. Blood and bullets were winning the West, and even though those sleeping couldn't feel it, the world spun just for them.

《《《 — 》》》

The morning air was chilly. The damp humidity slugged The Ghost in the face. Chalky tramped through the long fields of black grama grass and down into the valleys with the sweet smell of the wet mesquite. It must have rained here in the last day or so. The mud was thick where the grass wasn't.

They crossed a staggering array of landscape nearing the west Texas/New Mexico border. The cacti acted as prickly companions along the way while the soundtrack of the natural world cheered The Ghost along.

Hawks flew overhead. The snakes slithered along the rocky terrain, looking for a mouse to feed upon. The cold, clear water of the Rio Grande was close as the Organ Mountains peeked through the blue haze. The Soaptrees and the Creosote bushes grew in number, the cap rock mesas loomed in the foreground—he grew closer.

When he pulled into Las Cruces, The Ghost practically fell off his horse. Both were tired and beat. The Organ Mountains sat as a backdrop to the dusty little town. Peasants skirted along while shots rang out in the distance. The sound of rustled cattle mixed with the braying of donkeys and the whips of their masters in anger. Grabbing his saddlebags, The Ghost took a moment to pet Chalky. For a few moments, he watched her slurp up great mouthfuls of water.

«« — »»

He stood in the lobby of The Centennial Hotel. The snobbish clerk looked him over, and sighed before taking The Ghost's money.

Feeling he was being slighted, The Ghost made sure to spit in the spittoon like a local redneck, ensuring the man's unease as he was a pink, clean man in a dusty, violent cow town. When The Ghost paid, he felt the clerk's disappointment. It was apparent, his kind wasn't used to getting rooms in this fine establishment, which suited The Ghost. The hotel was an upper crust affair. No girls hung off the balcony nor was anyone gambling.

The wood was a dark oak and whatever master carved it did a terrific job of showcasing his skill with the ornate designs in all of the banisters and railings. The hotel smelled of fresh cut flowers and expensive soap.

«« — »»

He sat in the parlor of the inn, having dinner, when a man in a tan-colored hat, and a Silver Star on his shirt reading

SHERIFF approached him. He stood in front of The Ghost with his arms folded. The sheriff was tall as a big glass of piss and full of the vinegar to match. His store-bought confidence radiated through the paper tiger veneer he'd worked so hard to master.

The Ghost's head moved upwards, meeting the sternness of the eyes of the Las Cruces sheriff. The Ghost untucked the napkin from his collar. He wiped his mouth.

The Ghost leaned back in his chair.

"Hidy." The Ghost offered.

"What're you doin' in my town?" The sheriff answered.

"Well, that's a pleasant way to make friends. But, for your information, I'm here on personal business. What's it to you?"

"I know who you are," The Sheriff said through his frown. "You're the one they call The Ghost. Hear you bring nothing 'cept death and trouble wherever you go."

"Plenty of folks prefer a bullet to a judge."

The Sheriff clicked his heels, and looked around the room. He tried his hardest to play his cards cool, but it was obvious as the sour look on his face he had it in for The Ghost the moment his ass planted down on the chair seated in front of him.

The Sheriff lowered his voice, and his eyes.

"Las Cruces a peaceful town." The Sheriff pointed his finger at his star as if to signify he was the sole reason for Las Cruces' quietness.

He continued on his soapbox. "No one here is up to no good. I'd have them out of here if there were. I run a clean town. No whores, no gambling. No late nights. No need for bounty hunters."

"This place? You sure we're in the same city?"

"Since I've taken over, I cleaned up a lot of the filth that used to roam. No more."

"Sounds like a lot of No Fun if you ask me."

"Think you're funny?"

The Ghost lowered his eyes, and gave the sheriff something to chew on.

"I can be downright fuckin' hilarious." The Ghost went cold. "I'm here on business. If you've got a problem, that's your own doing. I'm here on a warrant set by the honorable G. Nazarko out of Texas. Contact him if you like, I'm official. I'm hunting men with bounties. Sheriff…" The Ghost held out his hand. The sheriff's arms remained tucked.

"Sheriff William Mehane."

Putting his hand down, The Ghost took the disrespect and filed it away. "Remember, Sheriff MeHane, there's a reason you know my name. Consult your local wanted posters once in a while. No place on earth is safe. Nobody within a mile knows yours. Wonder why?"

"We're a nice place filled with honest, God-fearing Christians. Why would you ever think one was afoot around here? I'd of been on top of it, Godmanit!" The sheriff grew frustrated at the insinuation of anything percolating under his nose.

"I don't know you from Adam. So, let's leave it at I'm here looking for one who deserves to be killed. End of story. You can't arrest me, and you can't make me go anywhere or do anything. You haven't got the power, or the guts. You're on my team—or you're in the way."

The sheriff was cornered with logic.

He wanted the credit for those safe streets, and one day when this place was booming, he'd get a street named after him, or the kids of the future would get a day off from their lessons. People dying would make the papers, and as the population was on the rise, the sheriff didn't need any harmful press.

"Have it your way. You're right; you are a man of the law, I guess. I'm the sheriff of Las Cruces. I'll be waiting, and watching." The sheriff dared, rocking his heels.

He wiped himself off and took off his hat. His pomaded hair glistened. He rubbed the band inside the hat, and spoke toward The Ghost, trying to appear jovial and good-hearted to anyone watching.

"If a man deserves to hang, a judge'll see to it. Not you, as you're so heralded for. Anyone who knows your story knows you never bring anyone you're after in alive."

"You're right." The Ghost took a sip of his water. "I don't let them live." He took another swallow and adding for a finishing touch: "I'd like to finish my dinner in my lifetime."

《《 — 》》

The Ghost found out that his destination was in Mesilla, not Los Cruces. Luckily for him, Mesilla was the other end of Las Cruces. Beer joints bustled with cowboys passing through town and shouting through the doors. Pool hall balls clanked together, and the competing girls stood out in the doorways telling The Ghost he was adorable. Tipsy cowboys sang trail songs, and the bartenders kept them drunk. The lamps flickered in flaming unison overhead, showcasing the dirt; mud and the blood all etched into the footfalls many pairs of cowboy boots.

Madame Esmeralda's was a shining ivory beacon of cleanliness when everything else around was a drab earth tone or ill painted hutch.

It was a cathedral, so bright and unsoiled; The House of Fuck illuminated the night sky amongst a sea of cheap imitators looking to make a quick buck from those shooed away at the door. A large hombre in a tailored suit stood at the top of the stairs. This place wasn't for the common trash looking for a quick lay; this was the domain of big money, and big bosses.

Cortez and Hidalgo pulled off opening an exclusive, classy joint. No riff raff was even out in front of the door.

The Ghost slept late into the afternoon. He let his body get as much rest as it needed. He nursed one hell of a hangover making his senses go dog shit. When he drug his sorry ass out of bed, he took to polishing his boots, guns and through the ritual. The boots needed to be shiny; it would be one of the first things the toadies at the door would notice. A high dollar clientele wouldn't come roping through in dusty riders; they'd wear the good footwear.

The Ghost knew the kind Madame Esmeralda's catered to: politicians, buyers and sellers, stockbrokers, and anyone in the underworld who's built their empire big enough to sit at the adults table. His hair was shaggy, his face unkempt. His clothes were destroyed. He'd get a full clean up for this act. He owed it to these last two to kill them with class. His moustache would be trimmed, and prim, and his hair would be pomaded and set like a clock.

He'd restocked on guns and ammo. He'd gotten a new .22—his third of the trip, a new revolver for his belt, and plenty of bullets. His belt was reloaded, as were all of the guns. Mesilla was gonna burn. When he looked at himself in the mirror at the clothier, he looked at the tired face of a man who appeared far different than the one who's left the ranch all those years ago. He parked Chalky out in front of the whorehouse and wiped himself clean. Approaching the stairs, he felt the doorman's inner mechanics trying to decipher the man The Ghost was. Bad men didn't have credit in a place like this.

Alluring hydrangeas bloomed in front of the large central porch where suited men and knockout Mexican call girls laughed at private jokes. Off across the street, The Ghost heard the regular street trade shouting after him, pleading theirs was no better and at a fraction of the cost.

Reaching the door, The Ghost took off his hat. He squared up to meet the gorilla standing in a blue pinstriped suit. The door guy looked him up and down from his shoes up to his hair.

"Seven bucks, cabron."

Most girls cost that much, but the investment was worth it. Seven dollars to walk in the door was highway robbery in any other situation. The Ghost slapped the paper inside of the large bear paw and walked on.

"No funny business. I see them guns; we don't put up with fighting or stupid shit. Got one warning." The big bear called out. The Ghost waved a hand in recognition.

Even the door handle was shiny and golden, and as he opened the door, a gorgeous mocha-colored girl in a revealing maid outfit greeted him.

"Entrée Sir. May I take your coat?" She asked, bowing and crossing her long, firm legs.

The décor of the place was the gold standard. Every penny the brothers must have ever made was sunk into creating a world of opulence and decadence. A pig fresh from the smoker laid out in a far corner of the room while piles of hot crawfish and fruits surrounded the animal.

Men in high dollar suits sat with girls who looked like they'd been plucked from the finest crop in the entire country.

The girl's teeth shined white. Their makeup wasn't a smeared mess; the elbow high gloves they wore were fine and tight against their skin. They fanned themselves and laughed at the jokes.

An older woman draped in black and pink; the housemother, the woman who played the part of Madame Esmeralda met The Ghost.

She grinned wide and directed him to get comfortable. She motioned him to a couch to take a seat and get a drink before selecting his girl.

Nothing was out of place, and even though she'd been rode hard in her day, she was royalty amongst the movers and shakers.

The girls hid off in the corners with their "Daddies" cooed at the men's affection and sniffed the bouquets of affection. A few were there for eye candy while business was discussed. No sex, no strings, just distract the competition with their beauty. None of the girls took their eyes off their clients; trained to give nothing their full attention.

He'd have to pick out a girl. After a few sips, he moved on over to the waiting area. The parlor filled with conversation while a piano player glided through Beethoven as background noise. Outside, the bands were hot and radical, but in here the music was tasteful and kept low key.

The madam met him by the large winding staircase and standing along the steps stood a row of girls more beautiful than the queens of neighboring nations. Each girl decked out in her sparkling costume jewelry and a beaming smile. Another massive sentry stood with his arms folded. He made no eye contact. His feet were implanted in the floor, as he was an oak.

"Welcome, Mr.?" The madam inquired.

The Ghost bowed, holding his hat. The crown of his head shined. He rose up slow and met hungry eyes from the ladies.

"Mr. Appleton." He extended his hand. "Rode in this morning and wanted company before I leave town tomorrow. In on train business."

He needed someone who wasn't on the company take, someone on the inside, but not a working girl. None of these girls seemed to be on the level; they fucked for money, and that was their trade. The Ghost wanted the girl opening the door. The mocha with the long, lovely legs and beaming eyes. Her.

He faced back around to the madam and whispered in her ear. The look on the madam's face wasn't pleasant, her lips upturned at such bestial intercourse in this house of respect. He promised a handsome fee. In spite of her protests, she spoke to the help. Ultimately, the Madame agreed upon the community room. The door girl would meet him at the first door on the left with the large brass knocker. The madam clapped and excused the girls, despite their groans of protest. Walking up the stairs to the first room on the left, he smelled their flowery French perfumes trailing in front of him.

He made his way into the small room. It was elegantly decorated in purple and blue tones.

The door girl listened with wide eyes as her boss spoke in harsh tones. No man ever requested her. Too young to be a comfort girl back when she was a slave, this would be her first experience with a white man with the doors closed. She was a working girl, for this one client.

When she opened the door, there he was. His jacket folded on the bed, and he sat beside it. His face didn't look evil, but it kept certain bleakness to it.

Standing proper, the nerves overtook her. Her hands fidgeted. She bit her bottom lip. Her feet pointed inward as her black hose ran up her chocolate leg. The Ghost drank her in.

"What's your name?" The Ghost asked.

"Delilah," She whispered.

A chair sat near the door. The Ghost motioned for her to sit.

"Pull that chair close. I wanna talk to you a minute."

Delilah did as she was told with nervous, gentle movement. She drew close to the bed and looked her client over.

"Look here Delilah, I hate to break your heart, I ain't here to buy your ass. I need you to give me information. Real easy. I'll give you enough to tell this place to go fuck itself." The Ghost pulled his wad of money out and held it. The sheer volume of the bills fascinated Delilah's eyes; no one walked around with that kind of money.

"So, you just want to talk to me? No foolin' around. Just talk?"

"Yep. Need you to help me. Didn't bother with one of the other girls. They're in on the take. You, on the other hand, you got nothing to lose. I don't mean in a bad way, either. White folks been fucking your people forever. You don't have to lift a finger, and you'll throw a wrench into these people's lives. You'll get paid to do it. By a white man, even."

The memories of being whipped as a child came as well as the horror of seeing her father treated no better than a dog.

"Who are you? No railroad man comes armed like a cowboy."

"Didn't take you long to notice the guns. They call me The Ghost. I'm looking for two men."

Delilah crossed her legs and leaned in, feeling like a co-conspirator.

"Yeah, and who would it be? I see a lot of men in suits come and go at all hours."

"Two brothers. Mexicans, one has a scar on his face. From the stories I heard, they're not exactly what you call nice fellas." Delilah's face lit up with recognition.

"I know who you're talkin' about. We never talk to them. They come in and out at all hours. No one says a word to them. They'll bring girls up, but they never hang around or talk to anyone of us. As far as me and the other black girls go, we're left in the cold as to what goes down." She paused. Her eyes grew into slits as she racked her brain trying to remember what it was they called them.

"The Crow Brothers. They never look nice. We won't see them for a while, and then they pop in and out. They look like two cowboys from across the street. The one with the scar is mean as hell. They killers?"

"Let's put it this way: they're wanted for a reason, sugar. The Crow Brothers, huh?"

"They do you wrong?" she asked.

"More wrong than you'll know."

"Been there." She dug her toe into the fibers of the carpet.

Delilah went on to give The Ghost a complete breakdown of the layout. Room by room she explained where each guard stood.

There were five in total. One by the door, one in the main parlor, one by the kitchen, one who roamed and another who hovered in the congregation area. All kept pistols in their coats.

Beyond the grand staircase, the upstairs had a total of eleven rooms. Downstairs, beyond the parlor and the congregation room by the bar, there was a kitchen, two girls' rooms and an office where the cash was counted.

"Think one of the Crows will pop in tonight if I hang 'round?" He asked, peering out to where the horses stood at the ready. Chalky looked bored.

"It's Friday, so they'll be in to count the till if you reckon they're the businessmen behind all of this." Smart observation.

He'd lost track of the days long ago, so hearing it was Friday was news to him. When he held out the money to her, she looked it over like it was the greatest thing she'd ever seen.

The Ghost motioned for her to let herself out. She beamed and began to inch closer him.

"Oh no. We got business to handle. I ain't going down there lookin like we didn't do shit. They'll know something's up. You paid for what you needed. This is on me. Free of charge." She closed in on him before he said a word.

«« — »»

He dressed and checked each of his guns. His billfold was lighter from paying off Delilah. She slipped out after a quick freshening up, but first giving him a deep tongue kiss. Slipping his boots on, he was ready to get this show on the road.

«« — »»

The nighttime drunks were out wrecking whatever wasn't nailed down, so the sentries of Madame Esmeralda's were on high alert, making sure no riffraff made their way into The House of Fuck. He slipped on his hat. The door behind him clicked into place. Delilah hurried around playing catch up on her duties as the watchful eye of the madam studied her movements.

New faces entered the house. Delilah greeted them with a playful "Entrée" as she did when he walked in.

His fingers glided down the polished wood banister. The madam met him at the bottom of the stairs. She did the customary walk to the door, should he want to leave, and be on his way.

"Everything was excellent, I take it? You're pretty flushed and happy. Our little girl must have done a job on you. You look like you've fallen in love. I'll have to hire her as a call girl, after all." She took a quick turn to Delilah.

"Goddamned dandy." He chuckled a little, totally serious. "She was marvelous. If you wouldn't mind, I'd like to sit at the bar and enjoy the scenery for a bit? I'm a bit wore out. I'd like to drink a few whiskeys.

I'm in for one night, and this place has all a man needed. Food, booze and women!" He played in his best awe shucks townie voice. The madam nodded.

"Absolutely! Comfort's what we specialize in. We're full service around here. We cater to a man's needs.

Enjoy the company of our ladies and by all means sample the buffet, it's free for our customers. Your drink is on me since you've already bought one and a girl."

He took a seat off in a corner with a small table. The madam ordered him a whiskey.

She pressed her hands on her dress and watched over as he took a sip and cheers'd her even though she was without a drink.

"You need anything, I'm here. Otherwise, enjoy yourself."

"Peachy," The Ghost said.

He held out a bill for her trouble, and the madam walked towards it and stifled a smirk. Insurance. Taken care of but left alone.

The piano player slid through something funkier than earlier. He made it extra greasy with tickles of his hands. He cut left and right down the keys, murdering the up-tempo swing of his left wrist. The whiskey was smooth; it wasn't fire in a bottle.

He'd been eyeballing a blonde falling out her dress. She caught him watching and gave him a wink; letting him know it was ok he took in the show. Delilah made her way over once or twice, passing along what information she had.

She leaned in close as she dropped his whiskey to the table. Her brown eyes smoldered.

The Ghost sipped on his whiskey. He watched everyone. Men and women played a game with one another, the men dangled bits of opportunity and promise wrapped in dollar bills while the women had to smile and pretend to give a fuck to take it. Smooth transaction to slap on a fake smile for slime, but cash money is what kept a roof over your head.

The Ghost's seat was at a slight disadvantage; there was a large blind spot behind him. He debated ordering another whiskey but erred on the side of consequence instead of habit. Given his position, he had to keep sharp eyes, but this was the best spot considering the layout. Despite his best efforts of keeping an eye on the room, The Ghost felt the barrel of a pistol placed at the base of his skull.

"Move slow. Don't act like nothin' is wrong, cocksucker. Don't make a scene." A voice whispered hissed in his ear. The Ghost picked up his hat and rose to his feet. He tickled the .22 in his jacket sleeve.

When he turned around, Cortez smiled wide. The Ghost looked straight on at his scar. The man had balls. Next to Cortez stood two of the guards. Just as dumb-looking as the one at the door, these baby-faced killers breathed heavy under the weight of their suits. They pointed their guns at him. Their aim was low, trying to keep it cool from to the untrained eye. He'd have to wait this out; they'd hit him in the gut or the hip. Trying to fight off three men with a bullet in your belly was bad business. For the moment, they had him.

Cortez looked more back-alley handsome than The Ghost imagined him. His long mustache matched the impenetrable blackness of his eyes. He wore his hair parted down the middle and back.

"Heard you were lookin' for me? Well, motherfucker, here I yam." Cortez nodded, and one of the two guards grabbed each of the visible revolvers from The Ghost. The guard patted him down but didn't get the knife in his boot or the .22 hidden up his sleeve. The Ghost still had options.

"Move real fuckin' slow. I ain't fuckin' with my clientele over your sorry ass," Cortez said.

The Ghost said nothing and did as he was told. The three men followed him down a long hallway and toward the back of the house. The kitchen stirred with the help frying up something that smelled delicious. The Ghost guessed it might have been catfish. As his boot heels walked across the long, polished wood hallway, the harmonious unity of the dark skinned women enchanted their walk.

With each footfall, he felt like a man walking toward eternity to the sad songs of broken backs and whipped pride.

When they reached the kitchen, they kept going, out into the yard and out of sight of anyone. The moon hung in the night air, acting as the silent judge for all of the world's illicit behaviors.

They arrived at an oak with long arms extending out, tickling the air. A long rope sat below with a noose on the end. They were going to string him up.

"She ratted me out?" He gambled and lost with Delilah. He faced the three men who still pointed their guns at him. Cortez laughed.

"Cabron. You think that I never fucked her? I fucked every woman in this joint. They all love me. They call me Daddy roun' here and they mean it." The Ghost got a good look at the scar that drug across Cortez's face. That scar defined him; it lent a certain viciousness that might have not otherwise been there prior.

"Shoulda known. That's what I get for playin' guessing games."

Cortez moved forward and pushed the hat off The Ghost's head with the barrel of his gun. The two men got a real good look at one another, enemy against enemy.

"That little beauty is getting a raise." Cortez beamed. He was damn proud of himself for this moment.

"She's give me a gift no one else coulda. The Goddamned Ghost's head on a plate! Motherfucker. Every cowboy and thief in the land is gonna come through Mesilla lookin' to shake my hand, drink my whiskey and fuck my whores. Thanks to you, fuckface. I'm gonna be more than jus' a bank robber. Gonna be known as the man who killt you."

One of the guards threw the rope over the arm of the tree. The noose dangled there. The Ghost looked at the rope's opening, where his neck was going to fit. He swallowed his spit and tensed his muscles, hoping he'd get out of this.

Cortez pushed him back on his heels. He held his barrel at The Ghost's neck while one of The Ghost's guns hung in Cortez's belt. The Ghost raised both palms up. Walking backward, he stopped as one of the men slipped the noose around his neck. For the first time in his life, he felt the hardness of the rope against his skin. One of the goons slid the knot down; the rope was tight, cutting off the air.

Through his uncertain fear, The Ghost kept his composure. If he let on he was scared, they'd make it worse.

"Guessin' you've never been strung up before, huh?" Cortez circled him. The Ghost kept his hands at his side.

"This is a first. Usually, I'm on the other side of the rope."

"Honored to be your hangman. Unless you're a gato, better hope for nine lives, cause we fixin' to break your neck."

The two men wrapped the remaining slack from the rope dogleg and pulled. Cortez folded his arms and watched as the life was squeezed out of The Ghost. His body began to rise feet into the air. In a natural state of panic, his hands immediately went to the base of the rope, trying to slip a finger in for air allowance. Whoever tied the noose did an excellent job. He was no better than one of the countless crooks he'd hanged in the past. His feet jerked wild, his face became a terrifying shade of cherry.

One of the men called out: "When he's dead I call them beautiful black boots!" He added a chuckle to see if Cortez would share his sentiment.

"Don't worry boys, we'll leave this piece of shit naked and dead in the streets." He lowered his voice and looked The Ghost, struggling to stay alive, directly in the eye. "Take anything you like. Won't need it where he's going. Maybe he'll see his brother."

The Ghost's feet dangled a few feet in the air, and the boys continued to put their girth into pulling the rope. He had to think through the panic. Now was the time. They were all as good as convinced he'd be dead any moment now. Luckily for him, they were smug enough to let him die in his jacket. As the two boys put their back into taking him up even further, The Ghost reached out his right arm and fired a shot from the hidden .22 in his jacket sleeve.

The shot didn't hit one of the boys, but scared them enough to drop him back to the earth. The rope came screaming out of their grip. His body fell hard against the ground.

Coughing and wheezing, he rose quick enough to fire a shot directly into one of the guard's heads. Four bullets were left. Cortez screamed at him like a warrior in combat. He began firing at The Ghost. From the ground, The Ghost pulled off a shot to Cortez's shoulder with the .22—the blood sprayed out from the small bullet hole.

Three rounds left. When The Ghost rolled over, squeezing the trigger twice at the guard frozen in shock, he fell to his feet, dead from two to the front of the neck and side of the head.

Cortez turned heel and ran back into the house. The Ghost slid the noose off his neck, throwing it to the ground. He grabbed each of the guard's guns and went on the hunt. Cortez was a dead man.

When he walked back into Madame Esmeralda's, it was mired in chaos. Topless women ran through the halls while Johns struggled to pull up their trousers. Cortez ran through the house, pulling anyone and anything in the path of The Ghost. He walked slow and methodical, and when one of the guards attempted to get in the way, he took their heads off.

Cortez stood at the top of the stairs, firing a shotgun down at The Ghost. Two of the guards flanked him on either side, firing aimlessly. The Ghost grabbed a table and flipped it for cover.

One of The Ghost's first shots blew a cavern into one of the heads of the guards, the one from the door.

The opposing shots came at a quick succession. He cocked his hammer and swung around, firing fast at Cortez and the remaining guard. The shots came from both sides of the long hall. Scores of bullets wrecked everything in sight as the unskilled hand of the guard took sloppy shots.

The Ghost landed a shot in one of the guard's legs. He shot him right in the shin. The small eruption of blood jumped out of his body and destroyed the bone. The man's revolver fell to the floor. Cortez screamed to get up and fight like a man.

"Get up and fight you cur!" He shouted. The young guard clutched his bloody shin with tears in his eyes, having never been shot before. He rocked back and forth in the fetal position. Cortez's angry foot met him like a mangy dog. He demanded he rise and continue to fight. The wounded sentry refused. Cortez, standing above him pulled the trigger. Shot point blank for his weakness in battle. Cortez screamed. The Ghost paused his shots; the air was smoky and stunk of spent gunpowder.

"Who the fuck are you coming in my house? When you run out of bullets, I'm gonna cut your tongue out, and shove it up your ass!" He fired the last of the rounds in the shotgun. He threw it on the ground in disgust.

The Ghost listened to Cortez's weak tirade. Two men remained upstairs, Cortez and one last guard. The hand was in his favor. He'd chance it.

The Ghost walked up the stairs with guns drawn. Cortez fired from The Ghost's stolen peacemaker. A bullet nicked the side of The Ghost's cheek. A trickle of blood ran down. Cortez dropped the spent gun. The mansion was empty except for them. Cortez dove into an open room. The Ghost followed behind Cortez and kept his pace even.

"The Red Seven are dead." He leveled his gun and fired at Cortez. He nailed him in the shoulder as Cortez managed to get a shot off at the same time.

Cortez's bullet sailed through The Ghost's arm. A clean shot. It spun him on his heels. Another wound in the already war-torn body. His fingers went numb.

Cortez yelped from the pain in his shoulder. The Ghost stalked him. He saw the working brain of Cortez as he moved closer.

The room was magnificent and massive. The balcony doorway was open. Cortez threw any piece of furniture to block The Ghost's path.

Cortez fired again; this shot sent The Ghost diving to the floor. Cortez fired as The Ghost was on the other side of the bed, using it for cover.

"I'll rip your heart out and shit in your chest, you piece of dog puke! You wanna come up in here and kill me? Better keep trying cabron, cause I ain't going down like a bitch. Guns up." He screamed toward The Ghost. He'd made it to his effects. He loaded the chambers of his revolver. Cortez's barrel snapped back into place.

"Come on motherfucker. I got six bullets to put you down. I pissed on your brother's smoking body after lit him on fire. You know that asshole? Fight me like a man, and quit hiding behind that bed you sack of shit."

The Ghost popped up quick and fired two shots laced with anger. Crooked. They missed. He went down behind the side of the bed.

"You said you killed em, eh? Serves em right. You wanna dig this grave? Get up and let's do this. I ain't scared of you. I don't care what the fuck they say. Get up and fight me." Cortez moved closer toward the bed. Each step was planned and even though he wasn't wearing shoes, he tried to be quiet, concise with each movement. The blood from his shoulder wound dripped down his exposed midsection. He licked his lips while a lone bead of sweat dripped off his chin. Droplets of blood stained the fibers of the carpet. He took a running leap toward the side of the bed where The Ghost lay and pulled the trigger. No one was there.

The shot blew through the wall. Turning, Cortez looked to his left and right to see if he'd missed the son of a bitch slither away and out the door.

From under the bed, came a slash in his ankle. The Ghost's boot knife severed the flesh where the ankle meets the Achilles. Instantly, blood spilled, and Cortez fell from the sharp pain. Cortez fired under the bed. The bullet hit The Ghost in the back of his calf. Tally another one. In turn, The Ghost shot from under the bed skirt and sank a shot in Cortez's foot. Crawling out from the other side, The Ghost hobbled over to the dresser. Dark blood spilled from his wounds. Once again his new clothes were ruined. Cortez popped up from the side of the bed where The Ghost was. He fired another shot; he broke the window.

Cortez stood up, his teeth gritted. Blood and sweat covered his face. Blood stained all over the once lovely carpet. The room was a patchwork of bullet holes, upturned furniture, and crimson DNA. The Ghost sized Cortez up; he mentally willed himself to see this through. His body ached from the beatings, bruises and gunshot wounds he'd received like a vicious baptism.

The Ghost didn't draw fire. They held their weapons out, circling one another. Cortez inched his way to the balcony door. The Ghost played it cool and waited for the opportune moment. Cortez knew the balcony was an escape route, but The Ghost saw it as an easy kill. Cortez dangled his fingers; he sucked the spit off his lips. It was time to make the move. He leaped off his heels, diving through the doorway, and as The Ghost took another shot from one of the revolvers, it missed.

"Told you, I ain't an easy kill. You came for me, and you're gonna have to earn this hide. I didn't care, and still fuckin' don't. You're outta bullets there, hoss. I'm gonna rip your head clean off your neck."

People shouted outside; many watched from below while others in the bars across the street were oblivious and lost in their drinks.

The balcony doorway was a few feet away. Cortez's palms grew sweaty. He debated on which move to make. It was either dive through the balcony door or try to buy time. Two definitions of duality stared deep into one another's beings. In one another they saw the antithesis of themselves. They couldn't understand one another any less, but it didn't matter—the bullets in their guns and impending death was the great equalizer.

The Ghost felt a surge of energy course through him. He took a step forward, ready to dance with the devil.

Cortez fired his last shot. He missed from a shaky will along with shakier hands. Cortez saw a world trapped in the flames of discontent. Cortez had one move left. He had to invest wisely which way to play this hand. Either run straight into the bullets of The Ghost and hope he'd knock him to the ground and rip his neck out with his bare hands, or get out onto the balcony and take his chances with a jump.

Holding the dead weight of the revolver, he threw it at The Ghost. Within the milliseconds of The Ghost moving out of the way of the twirling firearm, Cortez made his move out the door and to the balcony.

Cortez couldn't get far from the ankle cut and the bullets he'd taken. A small snail trail of red led out onto the virginal white balcony. Cortez managed one leg over the front of the railing as a small crowd of onlookers stared with mouths agape. Their fingers pointed as the shirtless, bloody gangster hung in the balance as this man came at him with guns pointed.

"What are you gonna do? You ain't gonna plug me and let me fall to the street. Come on bounty hunter, where are your cuffs? I'm worth more alive than I am dead. So, let's get this over with."

The Ghost leveled his black revolver toward Cortez's face.

"No bounties, no rewards," He said, pulling the trigger. Cortez's body fell into the dust twenty feet below. People gathered around with the blood seeping out of the holes in his body and married to the dirt below.

HIDALGO

Hidalgo sat alone in the office of the whorehouse. After the massacre, the Marshall shut it down for the time being, not that anyone would want to go inside it anyhow. A bottle, a pistol and a bowie knife sat on the rickety table. The bottle was half empty, but his glass was full. The tip of the knife was held in place by his index finger as its handle base spun against the wood grain of the table. No music played. He'd cried his eyes out over the death of his baby brother, and it sunk in: The End.

The riders of the gang, The Fixer, Snake Eyes and Danny Boy—his comrades in battle, his thieves in the night, brothers in arms, preachers in torment, and confidants in sin—all dead. Worst of all, the one that stung the most was his brother. Knowing that Cortez was gone felt like a knife to the gut, no matter the drinks he took from the bottle, the pain only grew.

He'd gotten word about Danny Boy a while back. No one said it was The Ghost. People die, that was just life. He'd been gone a few days, out scoring new faces for the brothel when he got the news. While a pang of sadness jolted through, it wasn't something he'd lose sleep over. Wasn't the first friend to catch an untimely end, it was just the outlaw way of life.

Hidalgo was in Las Cruces seeing his mistress as the gunplay erupted in his building. When he returned, his brother was dead.

It was chilling. In a world full of men like him, he was a man without a town, a country and nothing except an acidic, fleeting few hours here on the Big Blue Rock. Finality was in the air. Death imprinted the walls of this house.

Hidalgo's heart broke again. His brother was full of holes in the undertaker's office at the edge of Las Cruces.

He wiped the snot coming out of his nose along his arm, the mucus caking in the long black hairs. Running was pointless. This man was possessed by the notion of his head on a pike in the middle of the desert. Wherever he hid, it would serve as a bandage on a seeping wound. He was their leader, he was the man who made the decisions and with an iron fist. It was his idea they collect on The Ghost. In his money- and power-hungry youth, he wanted the world to remember one thing: The Red Seven were never caught. They were vicious till the very end.

Hidalgo took a lung-burning pull from the glass. His mind wandered over his life. He remembered his mother, full of scars and with unkempt witch hair welcoming horse faced men with no teeth into her bedroom from many towns over. He and Cortez never knew their fathers.

When a vengeful customer cut her up Jack the Ripper-style, the boys were left to fend for themselves. And by The Grace of God, they learned how to steal a horse, shoot a gun, and slit the necks of loose-lipped stoolies that flapped their gums. He too knew pain, he knew what it was like to fight for a scrap of bed as he and Cortez made their way into the Arizona territory, and over in New Mexico as faux wagon trainers. They made a buck any way they could, right or wrong side of the law.

Once the war was in full effect, they kept out of the conflict and worked breaking horses for the South out in New Mex.

They picked up jobs running guns or finding special needs for the men on the front line. Sides didn't matter. Money mattered.

When enough black powder couldn't get to the troops fast enough, the Crow brothers made it happen. For that, they were loved. Love burns out, and when the North claimed victory, the lifeline of the Crow brothers flat-lined. Making a buck whatever way possible became their game, and as both Yankees and Rebs started to bleed west into the interior, the West brewed with perfect chaos; the Crow brother's specialty.

Danny Boy came first. The kid they'd picked up along the way clicked at their heels, jawing how he was tough and how if they needed a boy to do the small stuff, he was their guy. Cortez hated him at first, but after a while, he made himself vital as he was willing to get his hands dirty.

The Fixer was the hired gun they'd picked up around Atlanta. Nothing but dumb muscle, he was an enforcer who rode in the middle of the pack and never complained, and never spoke up. He was a true menace, an ex-reb angry at the world for the plight of being born.

Snake Eyes was a New Orleans freak with a terrible taste for wanderlust, and extreme violence. The ranks of their little tribe swelled to five. It would be a while before they picked up Phineas along the California ridgeline. Desperate as a wild dog for food, that big brain of his kept them fat with a job and schemes to make a few coins. They acquired the Indian last as he was strung up for beating a man with a moose horn.

The seven of them rode across the lands, pistol whipping and punch throwing their way through dusty one-horse towns, and through the great cities of the north. From rape to robbery, The Red Seven killed men in the hundreds while stealing thousands of dollars from armed cars, trains, banks or plain anyone with a cent in their pockets. They stalked the land from top to bottom, corner to corner. The black joy in his heart didn't wane the reasoning for his demise.

The soft light of the lamp moved as the flame swayed like a belly dancer. Hidalgo's revolver lie in front of him, its blue steel tarnished from constant use and the harsh elements. Like a prisoner sitting the evening before he was scheduled to hang from the gallows, Hidalgo let life sink in.

Tomorrow, he'd meet his fate in the streets of Las Cruces. There was no other way. He was their leader, and as all of the men who'd ridden under him were with the angels, he couldn't run. He took another sip from the glass and let the silence of the empty house comfort him.

«« — »»

The Ghost lay in bed, his body sore and mind tired. He was full of bandages and desperately needed more sleep. He enjoyed not moving when he heard a knock on the door. Closing his eyes and letting out a yawn, he hoped it was his imagination. A second rap came. A gun was on each side in case one might be so bold as to venture in and play avenger.

"Come in." He cocked the hammer on his black revolver.

Taking his hat off, Sheriff Mehane walked in and stood at the edge of the bed. The Ghost looked up at him with sleepy eyes.

Sheriff Mehane whistled and clicked his tongue.

"Thanks for sending the boy over to the sheriff's office with a bloody scalp. Real class act you are. Heard your Shoot Em Up routine went over real nice in Mesilla."

The Ghost smiled. He was under Mehane's skin. He hadn't noticed in their last meeting; the sheriff had a long scar from his lip and around his left eye. It was one of those scars with a story. Childhood mishaps didn't leave a mark with a signature. A scar like that meant something.

A bottle of whiskey sat on the floor next to the bed. The Ghost grabbed it and pulled the cork with his teeth. He took a long drag and offered the sheriff one. Naturally, the sheriff declined. Shrugging his shoulders, The Ghost re-capped it and set the bottle down.

The sheriff's eyes drifted upwards as he took a long sigh and flicked his index finger at the bottom of his boots. He sighed again.

"I have powerful men here on train business, one of them read about your shenanigans. According to him, you're a Big Star in some respects. People know about you. Well, those who read the newspapers. Real nice. They want to make you more famous for killing off a gang that's defunct. While I understand the benefit to society, you're doing nothing except lending credence to the idea a gunslinger can be headline news, and for you to hunt them; they're bigger and badder. See my point?"

"I reckon I don't."

"You, Mr. Ghost, are causing a scene. I want you quiet as possible. I want you to be *The Ghost* and stay out of the way of any man who looks like he's got a dollar to spend. Las Cruces has a chance of rivaling Kansas City or even one of the cities in the north if the right people get behind us, and I ain't about to let some two-bit headliner steal my thunder. I'd blow your brains out if I could." The Sheriff stamped his foot for extra emphasis. The Ghost was unfazed by his cockamamie showboating.

The Sheriff spit on the carpet, defiant of The Ghost's room.

"Thanks. You're too kind."

The Ghost's arm swung over. He pulled the trigger on the revolver. The sheriff's mind splattered the black and yellow wallpaper with a thick layer of cardinal.

He'd explain the situation to the hotel manager, going with the lie that when he shot a man, it was for a reason. The real reason being the sheriff was a piece of shit.

He'd already killed someone, and it wasn't even noon.

The mid-morning sun was awful. Las Cruces boiled in its skin. The Ghost leaned against the hotel porch's pillar with a cigarillo hanging out of his mouth. He chewed the end while the smoke drifted off the cherry. The local doctor came by and tended to his wounds. He strongly suggested The Ghost remain in bed, given his condition. Naturally, The Ghost ignored his instructions.

He waited for Hidalgo. It was only a matter of time before the brother found out. Could be today, tomorrow or next week, but he'd come for him just the same. The Ghost stood on the porch of the hotel for a while getting some air when a boy came to the hotel with a piece of paper for him.

Let's get this over with. Meet me before sundown at the far north edge of town. Alanzo Street. Behind the church. I reckon one of us will need Him. We'll settle this once and for all. You want me dead, and I want to blow your brains out for killing my brother.

Hell's coming. You ready?

-H-

The Ghost folded the paper and stuck it in his pocket. Hidalgo was quicker than he expected. Not even 24 hours had passed, and here he was, ready to pull triggers. The Ghost spat on the ground and looked off over the rooftops. The sky wasn't even blue today, as it too was lost in the vacant heat of the desert. He made his back into his room and stood in front of the mirror. He was a terrible mess: bullet wounds and broken stitches.

The hour approached as the sun neared further to the West.

Standing over the washbasin, he wiped his face clean and ran water through his hair. He put on his jacket. A few days ago it was a new, high dollar piece of fabric. Now, it was laced with bullet holes and a layer of grime that wouldn't come out with any amount of elbow grease.

He took one last look in the mirror and pulled his gun again. He beat the reflection this time.

«« — »»

When he stepped out into the streets the world felt slower; the sun moved behind the clouds while creation lagged for a few seconds. He grew anxious. A burnt sienna hue kissed everything.

Women made the sign of the cross while gunslingers spit wads of black on the ground talking big to their friends. Their friends hit the bottle or stared at the red and black numbers on their cards, bored with the bullshit talk slithering out of their stupid friends.

The small white church was a few blocks away, and as he drew nearer, an overwhelming sense of calm came over him.

He would see this through, and he would do it with a mind free from distraction and hatred. At this moment, rooted in atrocity, it was up to him and right a wrong and use fluidity to find his movements and fast draw. If he let his anger blind him, Hidalgo would draw quicker. The spire of the church stood above the roofs of the other buildings.

The large iron cross appeared like a mile marker to sacrifice as he rounded the corner. It was quiet.

His hands hung at his sides while his fingers danced. No birds sang, and no one shouted his arrival on the scene. Even the wind held its breath. When he came to the lot, he saw them.

Hidalgo stood in the middle as two hired goons who looked a few evolutionary steps out of the gene pool flanked him. Two Mexicans with boot black tans, and tattered clothes.

One wore a large mustache while the other a scarred face and greasy skin. He must have pulled them from the depths of the drunk tanks, or they owed him a debt. These were bottom-rung hooligans with no stock in Hidalgo's game. The Ghost saw an idiotic sense of confidence in their eyes. In Hidalgo's eyes, stood a man without fear. A man ready to die. They stood twenty feet apart. All four men's fingers tickled the butts of their weapons, sizing one another up.

"I see you brought friends."

"Insurance policy. You're fast. I figured one of us might kill you. Three times the bullets."

The Ghost looked at the two men standing as security with hard eyes.

"Boys, this ain't your fight. I'd hate to kill you for no good reason. Defending this scumbag ain't gonna get you nothing 'cept a trip in a pine box."

The man with the mustache stepped forward and put on his best confident voice.

"Pendejo, I'll fuck you up."

The man went for his gun, and before his tips touched the handle, The Ghost fired one quick shot. Faster than jackrabbit cum, he was re-holstered and standing at the ready. The scar face man looked scared while Hidalgo's poker face was incredible. One dead.

"Impressive. Seeing your speed for myself is real nice. Why do you want me dead so bad? It won't bring anyone back. I'm just another body to add to the tally. Let's be men and walk away before one of us gets hurt?" Hidalgo gave him lip service, being condescending. The Ghost didn't play his game. This ended here.

"You ruined my life."

The Ghost fired at the second hired toadie. One more body on the pile.

It was the two of them. The way it was intended to be. Hidalgo didn't even bother looking at the two bodies at his feet. The two men's eyes stayed glued to one another. Hidalgo walked in clockwise as The Ghost went counter. The world remained quiet as the sound was the small rocks crushing under their feet. A hawk flew overhead and let out a screech echoing between the buildings and through each man. A signal. Both men drew their weapons and fired.

PHINEAS ALEXANDER

He'd ridden the Goodnight-Loving in the past, chasing the likes of men wanted for robbing stagecoaches along the Overland Mail Trail. The Ghost had ridden Chalky long through the Llano Estacado, and across to the weaving Pecos River.

Following the Pecos was a must if you wanted to stay alive. For miles, a man could go hours without seeing a drop of water. Carnage dotted the landscape along the Goodnight-Loving between the feuding cattlemen, and the unsavory criminals looking to sink a blade into a victim at the next watering hole.

It took a few hours ride to get to the town of Pecos from Las Cruces. The Goodnight-Loving Trail was hellish and cruel. It was an odd section of land to rustle cattle along, but many ranchers used it despite its hardships. He was sure, given the brutality of the trail, the medicine show would make the jump over to the Chisholm where towns sprung up daily. Towns would be far and few between for the duration of the ride. Those along the way would be ripe for the picking. The liar and the Indian; smart move was selling the salt of the earth their bottled bullshit falsities.

The Goodnight-Loving was a rugged cowboy trail, and it was a mapped crossing to make it up to the Colorado and Montana territories.

After the first hundred or so miles, The Ghost remembered why he hated The Goodnight Loving: the terrain was unfriendly, and the sun stabbing his body didn't make it any easier. The ride was rough, and as the land's natural inhabitants watched from under the brushes while vultures and bottom feeders circled in the sky as The Ghost and Chalky accrued miles.

The scene overhead was a malignant array of destructive colors pummeling one another into a bruised violet submission, bleeding across as far as the eye saw. The Ghost felt at one with the striking panorama. After the blood spilled post-Civil War, blue and Grey-backed bodies lay face down in their remission while men behind desks made dramatic choices of their doom for them. Men wanted this land and rightly so—the mysteries of the ages lie out in the cradling landscape. The Ghost saw the soul of a fractured America in this land.

Soon, he'd run into a team or two running cattle as the major herds in their massive swells headed north to the slaughterhouses. The sun was upright in the sky at its full, murderous height. His body was covered in a fine film of salty sweat. Soon, he'd reach Dead Horse Crossing, and the water, although dangerous, would feel amazing.

He took the arroyos and the barren brush fields at a comfortable trot, riding Chalky to death in this hellish climate would break the horse.

He'd moved into a valley where patches of mesquite dotted the caramel landscape. It was around midday when the rumble of many horses came from behind. A broad swath of shirtless, tan riders headed toward him.

They glided down the knoll, and into the valley, moving like a school of fish in the eastern sea. It would be foolish to try and ride off.

He'd make the situation worse by dishonoring them. The Ghost stood his ground, ready to die on the back of his horse like a man, facing the living ghost's of America's sanguine past.

Over the years, he'd shared his run in's with the natives, and he'd been lucky to meet with them under favorable terms thus far. He left the Union's ranks after being designated for Indian killing patrol. That was a line he refused to cross.

The Ghost remained stoic as the pack of stone-faced warriors surrounded his horse. Covered from three sides, they stood above in the mesquite, arrows at the ready.

A dozen or so of them engulfed him; probably out on a hunt or keeping an eye for a herd to steal a cow. The land opened wide beyond these hills, this spot was the perfect place to hide, and wait.

The rustling cowboys wouldn't let them cherry pick their pieces of commerce, but they certainly wouldn't want to deal with a full-on Indian attack, either.

Chalky danced nervously as the army of pintos and Appaloosas gathered all around with their feral eyes upon it. The men atop their beasts said nothing and didn't pull their weapons as their leader rode in. He was quiet and without pretense. Context forms content.

Luckily, they were Apache. While they weren't pleased with the pale skinned, land-stealing hombres, they let a man speak his peace. Comanches never granted such. Anyone who didn't exist in their common code of violence was dead where they stood. Warrior code.

The leader moved in closer.

"What are you doing out here? White skins are not welcome." He spoke English, a good sign.

The Ghost knew not to even try a song and dance with the natives; they saw through the lies many white men laid upon their people, and their trust was paper-thin to begin with. He'd have to give it to them straight.

"I'm on the hunt for some men."

"You are a killer of men?"

"Could say that. Looking for a traveling medicine show featuring one of your enemies, a Comanche, who likes to cut people up. He and his gringo companion murdered my family. I aim to take their heads clean off."

"Who is this Comanche?" Their leader asked.

The Ghost sneered saying his cancerous name.

"Name's Charley Warchief." The Ghost let the name hang for a second and spat to signify his disgust.

The Apache leader's eyes shot to each of the men flanking him to the left and right. They gave approving nods. The Ghost continued. "Used to run with a gang called The Red Seven. Currently, he's with a Medicine Show, claiming to be a hoodoo man witch doctor. I intend to blow his brains out."

The Apache leader held his hand up and spoke.

"I know the man you speak of." The Apache leader said before calling out to one of his men in their native tongue. The others parted as one warrior strode forward, joining to the side of the chief.

The man's chest was a terrible array of slashes and scars. His tanned hide couldn't hide the odd, white colored cuts and scar tissue built up over the years. It was like he'd survived a bear attack.

"This is Midnight Fox. He was lucky enough to survive one of the battles with Charley Warchief out in the hill country. He is a proud Apache warrior. Survivor of many firefights with our enemies of all creeds. Midnight Fox's father shares my blood. When my nephew came to live amongst our tribe, he told the tale of a man so cold he saw the gringo's devil in his eyes."

The warrior pointed at the markings on his chest while the leader spoke. "They say his teeth point like a wolf's, and he scourges like a starved coyote. His heart craves to be with the noble lobo, but his soul is too wicked. This man slaughters all, regardless of skin. He left our people to be with the white man and has battled against his people. But now he kills with a gun, not a club."

The leader wiped his mouth and spat in disgust. "His name is known to anyone who's battled Comanche. He's said to drown a man in a buffalo hole. Letting the rough water be his last breath." It was more appealing to get your guts ripped out and danced upon than spending your final moments sucking in bastions of disease and filth.

"When a war raged between Apache and the Comanche out in the midlands, this man lay for dead under his horse. As he opened his eyes, he was not dead. Many bullets were said to be inside of him. To survive, he cut open the belly of his dead horse, and drank the water. They say he's eaten the flesh of his enemies to gain their powers. This man, he is a demon. He will break you if you let him."

The men locked eyes. The gooey paint streaked across the Apache's eyes glistened in the sunlight. It was red, the color of blood, and redemption.

"We are not enemies of your people, but your people have given us no reason to trust them. I see you are not an evil man. I can see evil in the hearts of many, even my own people. I can see the song behind your eyes. But know, this man will show you your heart before you die. There is no good within him. He kills because there is more reason to suffer than to love. Know he would rather do it with his fists. One thing I can tell you: his right eye is dead. There is no color. When you strike, strike to the right."

The Ghost swallowed hard. The idea of fear was isolated to the battlefield and feeling a ball in the pit of your stomach when a singular moment of redemption was yours, if you could pull the trigger when you knew a man in the opposite colors was at the ready, waiting to take your life the same.

He didn't fear the living man, no—he feared what Charley Warchief *represented*.

«« — »»

In the distance, an owl signaled to the night it was open for business. He imagined himself on the land with Annabelle in tow. Her unrestrained, devilish beauty radiating long beyond the fields of green bathed the Masterson family ranch. Her genuine, warm glow made him feel comfortable in his skin. She wasn't impressed with scoundrels with cash-lined pockets as New Orleans was prone to, nor did she ever let him take a pass for free.

If she desired his heart and soul, she owned them, he liked that she made him earn it. Working for something was far more valuable than it being free without much fuss. He longed to speak to her again.

The alienation crept in more and more these days. The world out here was a silent storm. The nothingness echoed long, and the noises sounded cataclysmic usually draped in the wild silence. The smoke from the fire drifted upward, twisting into various shapes of deer, skulls, and a giant panther ready to attack.

That morning he'd started to get ready when he heard a loud trampling far off into the distance. He knew the sound: herds storming up the trail. Pulling out his spyglass, The Ghost observed as the gigantic swell of Longhorns stormed deep in the hundreds. Loads of cattle rushed up as a team of wranglers strode alongside, careening them on their route northwest.

There were eight men he saw leading the bovine band. Out a mile or so, if he wanted to, he could have caught up with them. Instead he let them ride in peace. He'd be running into a settlement, or town here in the future, and piece together what was what, and where he'd find his medicine show.

It was comforting witnessing the trail wasn't cold, and even though they weren't friends, he wasn't too far from other humans. Before he left the spot, he took out his boot knife and carved into a cedar:

Ride like Satan dangled his fork at your hide while the eyes of the south go far over the desert with violated pupils. Notice the madness of pride in the flags of dead men.

He reached Horse Head, or as the Indians called it, Dead Horse Crossing. The olive green water rushed at a frantic pace over the jagged rocks protruding above the liquid. The sound of the moving water echoed against the serene setting, despite wrapping itself into the arms of death at all angles.

Sun bleached horse skulls hung in the trees, daring anything breathing to enter at their own risk. This was the only point of the Pecos that was fordable, everywhere else along the way, the mud was too thick and the quicksand could swallow you whole. They called it "the graveyard for cowmen's hopes" because of its rough waters. Cattlemen accounted for a loss when they reached this point, no matter how hard they tried, they'd consistently lose stock, and worse off many lost their horses. But it was this or nothing. The precious few other less-formidable parts were typically along the Comanche Trail, and with that came a promised suicide.

If anyone wanted to get over toward the eastern side, they had to make their way past this point. Sure, you could find other points to cross, but you'd be going out of your way for hundreds of miles. Your animal would be dead by then.

The Ghost felt his companion tighten up. Many four-legged comrades's disheveled, broken faces dared it to do what they couldn't.

The Ghost knew to rest up. He hopped off and went to the water. The current was strong, and the water was the perfect cool. He took two handfuls and splashed his face, and through his greasy hair. His beard was fully grown, and the blistering Texas sun made it hotter on his face. He could smell the water's briny scent.

He rubbed his friend's long snout. Chalky took a long drink and seemed to be ok. His animal stood at the ready. The Ghost dug his feet into the squishy mud, and as he pulled his boots up, he felt the mud attaching itself, not letting go.

The footing was rough, and the thick mud would be hard to cross. He'd gone this far up the trail once. He was lucky enough to make it. His Appaloosa fought hard through the muck, the quicksand, and the ripping current. Luck was on his side that day. Today, he hoped, wouldn't be any different.

Looking at Chalky, The Ghost hugged its long face and held it next to his chest. He gave it a long set of pats on the head. The horse exhaled, and stamped its foot, ready to get on either dying in the water or traversing like a champion. The Ghost wished he could talk to it, and make it understand how harrowing this ford was to cross. Even though it was the easiest, and shallowest along The Pecos, it was a murderer.

They rode into the water. Instantly, he felt Chalky struggle against the quicksand and the strong current. He gave the horse a few small jolts to the ribs, and it muscled through the muddy bog. The water rose. It was electric and surging.

The water was up to the horse's head, its neck visible amongst the current. The Pecos was unforgiving as it rushed against him like the front line of the opposition.

His body shook, putting all of his weight into trying to control the struggling beast beneath him, yelling at the four-legged fuck to keep moving.

Like a general, he worked Chalky into a focused machine, desiring one thing: to beat the pummeling current. Every movement came close to knocking him off the horse he hugged tight. The other side of land was less than fifteen feet away. The horse struggled. Victory was upon their lips as the salty, liquid boxer took another shot and laid the master and his beast off their game.

The current drug him below. For a second, he floated weightlessly. The Pecos willed its liquidity upon him, trying its hardest to bash the breath free from his lungs. The river didn't just want his horse, but it wanted him, too. As he tried to find his head above the water, an invisible hand put all of its might down, and toyed with The Ghost; letting him know nature was a cruel mistress. He scrambled through the briny haze. He shot up, gasping for air.

His lungs and throat battled the layers of salt caking the airflow. His eyes burned, and as he spat up the water in his lungs, he thrashed the water, searching for his companion.

The Ghost tried to swim toward his friend, his ally. As its neighs became weaker, Chalky fought the rushing water that kept dragging him under. He was losing the fight against the elements.

With a great feat of strength, The Ghost struggled toward the shore. He intended to run along the shoreline to catch up with the struggling horse and dive in when he'd reached a point of safety to help his friend. The Ghost pulled himself within five feet of the shore with the force of the water beating down on him still.

He found his footing and fought toward land. His boots sank with pressure as he moved forward. He clawed his way toward the bank. Grime, sand and dirt embedded under the nails.

He'd lost the gun he kept in his belt, but his black revolver was snapped in place at his side. His black preacher's hat floated near the edge of the water.

He reached over and threw it a few feet away into the brush. The color and breath returned after a few moments of deep breathing. A few beats passed, and he was off his heels, screaming.

The Ghost ran up and down the riverbank, frantic and hollering for the horse. There was nothing.

The Dead Horse claimed another. Chalky wasn't strong enough, or smart enough to beat the conditions. The Ghost felt deflated, alone and defeated. Emptiness surrounded him.

All he had was the clothes on his back, a gun, the bullets on his belt, the canteen strapped across his back, and whatever folding money in his pocket. And his boot knife; he managed to keep the slasher during and after the war, and he'd be damned to lose it out here. His consort was gone, and so were his provisions.

The west Texas landscape was treacherous, and he was alone. Tears burned as he screamed out in agony. For the rest of the day, he wouldn't move from this spot, idiotically faithful his horse would rise from its watery grave. In his fantasy, they'd continue the journey together. From this position, the water looked serene and calming; even nature was a liar.

«« — »»

He rose at sun up. His boots were still damp, and as he traversed so many miles, his feet ached. His body grew stupid, and the sun did its job of robbing his already salt poisoned body crazy. His jacket was long gone, and he wore his sweat-soaked shirt, around his neck.

The Ghost's bodily functions failed. He needed fresh, clean water. Sweat dripped from the hairs on his face and into the steaming sand below. After some miles, he stumbled upon a tiny creek; The Ghost fell into the fresh water, and drank till his body couldn't anymore. He laid in the water and let the cool liquid soak into the fibers of his clothes. The kiss of the water across his skin felt divine. Every molecule in his genetic makeup made love to the components in this glorious drink. He felt like a pig jostling for comfort in the shadow of the slaughterhouse. When he rose, every inch of him was soaked. It felt good to absorb the loss of Chalky for those precious moments of life affirmation in the depths of the cool water, despite it only being inches not miles deep.

In the miserable heat of the barren country, his clothes became dry within a few miles walk. When the afternoon sun reached its peak position, slamming each inch of life it touched, The Ghost hid in a small scrub field of brush and mesquite. The shade wasn't much, but it was better than hustling across land hotter than the pits of hell on Liars Night. When the sun began to wane into the clouds, he moved again. His feet carried him as far as the dry body atop let them go.

A wild coolness hung in the night air. The breeze ripped through the once hot skin and stung in different primitive sadism. He took up for the night between creosote and faced against some large shale for wind blockage. His canteen was long empty, and between his hunger pains and the shellacking sun, he was fading fast.

He'd made it a few miles before he collapsed. His face hit the dirt. His mind traveled to familiar and wonderful places.

His inner voice promised death as he slipped off toward wherever it was where men go when they die. His breathing became slow and labored, off in his subconscious his brain spoke to his heart. *So this is what it's like to die.*

When his body rejected death, and demanded systems get in service, his eyes cracked open. He took a sobering look at the scrum around him. He needed to eat, and soon. If some gunshots, stab wounds, and a killer river didn't kill him, the sun worked against fate.

He rose to his feet and ambled over to a rock. His face looked terminal. He needed to hunt anything and cook it.

The Ghost sat quiet with his revolver drawn. He waited. After a while, a few yards away, a jackrabbit drew near. He'd have to rely on a steady hand, and pray some of that sharp shooter skill wasn't lost in this strained state. He eyed the jackrabbit scampering around, looking for its own dinner. He was fifteen yards out. His eyes shrank to slits, his lips pursed. He held his breath and squeezed the trigger.

The rabbit flipped as the bullet crashed through its skull. The Ghost walked over to his meal and lifted it by the legs.

He returned to his rock and looked the rabbit over. He was a muscular little scamp, so he'd be good eating.

It took a bit, but eventually he created a fire. Lucky for him, he was in the right environment where dry kindling and flint stone were aplenty. A spark caught a dried out bit of grass and before long a fire danced. He skinned the jackrabbit and placed it on a spit above the heat. His eyes watched the grease pop out of the flesh and coat the meat.

He'd sleep near the fire for a bit. Before sunrise, he'd make some miles. He wasn't sure how long he'd be able to last at this rate.

It didn't take long before he'd caught a sight of a small pueblo town off in the distance. He stood at a large ridge, looking like hell rode through, and on top of him for eons. The village seemed around three miles away. He hoped the walk wouldn't kill him. When he reached the town, it was a shoddy, lip curl of a place. Drunks sat on porches, bent down in their own vomit. Fat bellied whores looked out toward a missing clientele, while rheumy eyed scum sold goat meat from butcher blocks in disease ridden doorways.

A few pigs and sheep ran through the streets as dirty children ran around chasing one another naked to their waists or without any clothes.

Passing down the main drag of the little place, he found a small building.

It looked abused and unwashed, but whatever was being cooked smelled far better than his desert jackrabbit. Suspicious eyes followed him as he walked inside the little storefront shack.

The brown, toothless man sitting behind the ramshackle counter nodded as The Ghost took a seat. The Ghost looked like warmed over dogshit. The crusty old timer set a rusty tin can of water down. The Ghost drank it empty.

"Comer?"

"Si."

The Ghost's Spanish was mediocre at best. He knew enough to get a plate of food or acquire whatever goods he was in the Mercado for.

A few beat-looking men drifted into the joint and sat behind him. They wore tattered duster jackets and looked like they'd ridden from the end of the earth and back with beat red faces.

Red dirt caked on their brows while their hands looked rough and cracked. One looked like he spoke English, given his green eyes and red hair. There were three and looked rougher, or worse than The Ghost did.

The men said nothing to one another and replied in nods as the little toothless man took their orders.

A frail old woman appeared with a plate of steaming food. Her smile was broken, yet warm. He tore into what looked like meat. It could have been rooster, horse or house cat. It was indistinguishable, and without base to judge, it was the better option.

After he'd finished, and the men behind him took their fill, The Ghost faced them. He'd met enough rogues in his professional life to recognize the look of a rustler or scheming swindler.

"You boys know where a man can buy a horse?"

Turns out they were in fact a band of horse thieves. After ferreting out he wasn't on their ass for their crimes, they opened up shop. The stock they offered wasn't top dollar, but it would suffice.

In the end, The Ghost scored a shotgun, another pistol, and a tall, muscular sorrel. He paid a fair price, and the men were happy to take the money and ride out as soon as possible, headed down to Coahuila where they'd mark up the horses at a premium. The saddle he bought off them was a basic job; nowhere near the comfort of his custom piece sitting at the bottom of the Pecos, attached to a dead Chalky. Grabbing the horn, and swinging over and onto the horse. He spoke to the one with red hair.

"By chance you boys tell me where in all fuck I am? Was on the Goodnight-Loving and lost my Chalky down at the Dead Horse."

The man with the red hair spat on the ground before speaking.

"Ugh. That fucking crossin'. Many men lost their entire lives trying to ford that pass. Shit should be a bridge by now, but some asshole'd go and fuck it up anyhow." The man spit a slimy wad of chaw to the ground. "Yer bout ten miles off the trail. Yer due east of the Goodnight. Ye git here on foot by the looks of ya?"

"Yes, sir."

"This is a hard country on foot, friend."

"Wasn't easy. I can tell you. That there little old man's gruel saved my life. I was getting lost out there and I don't if I had much longer in me."

The other two grew antsy, wanting to get out of this little haunted town. It felt as if dead eyes searched them, and through them with each movement.

The Ghost didn't like it much either. But, he'd remain here for the evening. He'd stayed long enough out in the shit to appreciate a room over his head for a night.

"Lemme ask you a question. You spot a medicine show on your runs?"

The men looked one another over. Their poker faces stern. The Ghost felt change in their air. They knew something.

"I'll take your silence as a yes."

"Didn't say we did," the red head said. His other two companions kept their traps shut.

"Boys. You don't know me, but I know your type. We're all businessmen. I have a few extra dollars in my pockets. Those dollars are yours."

"We ain't snitches."

The Ghost pulled out a bill, and the eyes of the men lit up.

"This is where we're at: looking for a medicine show. Got a big Indian and a black haired thief running it. Real easy."

The men looked at one another. One of the other two men spoke up. His voice was shaky and frail. For such a mean face, what came out of him was puppy sized.

"If he ain't gonna play ball, I will."

"Glad to see one of you got sense. Keep talking and this bill is yours."

"They know you're coming. You're lookin' for Phin & The Comanche, ain't ya?"

The man gave way to a sickening grin. The Ghost nodded in recognition. The man continued.

"I knew it was you when we were in there. Only a psycho would be out here as beat up as you, and looking as mean. I thought you weren't real. I thought you were just a story. The Ghost as I live and breathe."

The man tipped his hat. The Ghost sat cool and nodded in recognition.

"They's heard you're on their trail. Someone wrote a letter. You've been killing their friends. I'll sell those sons of bitches out, though. They were supposed to buy a few of these horses off us. Since you're around, Phin, he's watching his ass like never before. Got two goons hanging round, lookin to bust heads. You best be rested up for a fight with his Indian. He'll rip you in half if you give him an inch. We lost money, them getting cheap on us. We been dealing with them over the years. We ain't friends. We do business. Phin may try to pretend he's a reformed man down from the mountain with God's word; it's a bunch of lies and nothing more. He's still a piece of shit."

"Sounds like you knew more than I gave you credit for."

"I may be a lot of things, but I ain't stupid. We go back a ways. We acquire goods and they buy them."

"Where are they?" The Ghost asked.

"Fifty miles due north I'd guess. Itty-bitty town called

Delgado. They're headed up to Colorado." The other two men moved uncomfortably in their saddles as the small voiced man laid it out.

"That on the Goodnight?"

"Yep. Following it to get the boys rustling cattle's hard earned money when the hookers and gambling dens aren't. Get on the trail and you'll run straight into them."

"How many men are with them?"

"The two of them. Two helpers, and whatever musicians and bullshit they've got running along. They ain't shit. The helpers are hired guns. They'll take a shot at you if you try and get at their leader. Expect to be killin' four instead of two. The rest of the bunch is harmless. They're out there making a way, like anyone else."

The Ghost handed the man the money. The man stuck it into his shirt pocket.

The Ghost rode the sorrel over to the burned out church. He led the horse through to the back where he tied it up. The thatched roof was full of holes from the fire, but it was a form of shelter. There was no inn in a dreadful town like this, and the church was sacred ground, at least enough for tonight, anyway. Dried blood stained the broken wooden pews while the iconography was broken and scattered. It was apparent people were murdered in this room. Disturbing reminders of the violence lie naked to the eye.

The town wouldn't be wrong to burn such a miserable place down when it was to re-populate.

He moved a broken pew over toward one of the walls and made a small fire on the floor. The church was dank; putrid moistness impregnated the air.

A great cheerlessness permeated the whole town, the church being the central beacon to sadness. This ramshackle town was haunted in the daylight.

He'd sleep in this battered shell of what was once a place of worship and dream of places far brighter and with more life than the current macabre den of terror.

At dawn, he rode fast and hard out of the little town. He'd be glad to never step foot in such a place draped in misery. It would take the better part of the day to get back on the Goodnight, and toward Delgado. He rode with the wind at his heels, and eyes focused on the road ahead.

He expected to see the devil himself thumbing for a ride as he and the sorrel left rocks and dust in their wake. The horse was much faster than Chalky; maybe they would get along after all. Till they reached Delgado, no rest for the wicked; there was a panic within The Ghost, and nothing would quell it.

When they descended upon Delgado, The Ghost and the sorrel were exhausted. It was around four in the morning when he stabled the horse. The sorrel buried its head in a pile of hay. Sweat dripped down the beast's neck. The Ghost found a room above a small bar. He slept like a stone.

Delgado in the morning hours was a bustling town on the Union Pacific railroad line. Steam engines rolled through loaded with passengers while trains delivering goods were short on the heels behind. Stores with the newest in couture lined the streets while places with signs reading: NO IRISH— NO MEXICANS—NO CHINESE—NO BLACK hung over some of the bars. The Ghost saw a place called CHINK's LAUNDRY that kept hogs. The Ghost knew what exactly those hogs were for, and it wasn't just for their bacon. When you needed a body gone quickly, men kept pigs. Toss the body in the slop and before you knew it, problem solved.

A beaten, washed over sign read HOUSE NIGGER & SERVANT CLOTHES—an indication of the attitude before the war when it looked like no end was in sight for the business of selling human flesh.

Delgado wasn't as bustling as the old streets in New Orleans, but it was eons ahead of the nightmare he'd slept in days ago. He'd located information on the medicine show from a low rent hustler who fancied himself a high dollar crime boss. The medicine show was camped outside the town limits and rumored to be riding out on the trail after today.

《《《 — 》》》

Phineas Alexander was a small, nebbish man. He wasn't a hangdog scoundrel or covered in grime and putridity. He was clean, almost dainty. His beady eyes sat deep in the snow of his white face. His hair was plastered against his head with a part straight down the center.

He always seemed scared, like a gunfight was around the next corner.

How he became a rider with the likes of The Red Seven was out of his shrewd business practices, and willingness to let other's who weren't so smart take their anger out on one who owed them money. He was a thinker, a planner, and a man who understood, calculated and capitalized on the schematics of a situation in the larger sense; Alexander applied his brainpower.

While a shoot 'em up gunslinger like Snake Eyes would be more than happy to fire on a bar in the name of revenge, or how

Danny Boy would rob and kill anyone for a few bucks, it was Alexander who'd piece together how they'd amass small fortunes without killing one another.

His mind didn't work like the average bum off the street, he planned and processed; he made them rich. In Alexander's head, he saw numbers and figures, not bullets and guns.

He felt no guilt or shame; people were commodities lending themselves to a systematic construct to which all perpetuity found it's way in the balance. The art of hustling for a few cheap dollars is what made Phineas Alexander's world go round, he liked to see deals close, and people suffer in the name of a dollar. He was a true business-minded sociopath.

The medicine show routine was easy money. The cost was low, and profit was sky high if you banked on prime theatrics. Sell the people the bullshit they wanted for their ailments with the promise of the God's of the savage Indian Charley Warchief, coupled with a little smoke and fire from the good white man's tonic of bullshit:

Jesus H Christ. Mix the two into a dark concoction of lies, and slight of hand, and before they knew it, patrons begged to be saved by this magical healing elixir.

The rule along the trail was twenty-four in a small town, and forty-eight in the bigger ones. Spending too much time in a town got you found out. They'd stuck with this routine for a while, but that changed after Alexander received the letter.

It was postmarked from New Orleans. From a stranger with bad handwriting named Holbrook, who claimed to be a friend.

He said there was news: The Ghost hunted The Red Seven. Alexander read and re-read the letter. His eyes stopped on the words The Ghost and The Red Seven. His past came back to get him. Alexander knew it was possible but realistic? Hardly, it would be a lot of work sussing out where they were. He, himself barely knew where they'd all landed these days. The Indian would have to kill him.

The letter went on to say The Ghost took out Danny Boy, Snake Eyes, and The Fixer. He wondered if The Ghost had made it to Hidalgo and his brother? Holbrook explained how Snake Eyes and The Fixer each met their deaths, in gruesome detail. The New Orleans papers sensationalized The Ghost once again. The man in black was back, and everyone in Louisiana squealed at the thought of the superhero coming to rid their town of evil men.

Alexander knew better, begging for attention was a mistake; The Ghost was methodical and deep. He may not have a plan right now, but he had a goal: to kill each one of the gang, and by that standard his legend was dusted off as the imaginations of the populace ran wild.

Fear trickled down Alexander's spine. When he let the Indian read the letter, the Indian closed his eyes and muttered nonsense about preparation and readiness.

"This man, he is a killer. We will die," Charley Warchief said after a few pauses between them. "What do you mean 'we'll die?' That's what I got you for! You're the muscle of this here outfit!" Phineas Alexander shouted. A small bit of sweat dangled between his bottom lip and chin.

"They call him The Ghost because he rides along with death. He was a good man made into the bringer of doom. You should not be surprised. He wants our souls. I have foreseen a pale horse riding into our lives. I must prepare to meet my grave. We took lives from him. He has come to collect ours in return."

Charley Warchief lowered his eyes until they were almost black holes, he chanted to himself. He dragged the lake of whatever crept inside as the rumbling in his chest, and mouth and throat grew louder. Alexander was beside himself with the coolness of the Indian. The man he'd known to slaughter anything, for any reason, seemed palpably cool despite an oncoming problem in the form of The Ghost.

"Prepare your fucking grave?! The hell's wrong with you? You're gonna get a few of these low life bastards together and blow his ass off the saddle before he can get near us! That's what you need to do, hoss!" Alexander spoke with a terrible phobia. Charley Warchief's face was stone.

"I dreamed of a bear chasing an elk through endless fields. The bear growled and screamed. Hunger kept him moving, and the elk was too fast. The bear, in all of his pride, wouldn't stop. He demanded his food lay down for him. But, the elk would not. If he was to die, he'd make his foe earn it. I saw myself in the eyes of that bear. My pride has led me here."

Alexander's mouth hung open.

"You mean to fuckin' tell me. A Goddamned dream about a fuckin' bear chasing after a fuckin' deer means you're just gonna call it a day and left this motherfucker kill us?"

"There is nothing I can do."

"I can't believe what I'm hearing. For as crazy as you are, you sure as shit ain't acting like no cold-blooded killer. I saw you kill a man over the hat he was wearing, and now, you can't take a swing against The Ghost? What in all fuck is going on here?!" Alexander stated, frantic.

"I will prepare myself to fight. He will seek me out. I will use all of the force of the Gods to extinguish his fire. This man was sent from the spirits. I will wait for him. I will challenge him. I will fight him. I will not give my soul with ease. I will accept dying from a real warrior such as he. It will be an honor dying by the hands of The Ghost."

"Are you listening to yourself? You're fuckin' nutty! You need your fucking brain looked at! How can I trust you when you're already ready to lie down and die? Might as well fuckin' throw dirt on you. You see a Goddamned nonsensical bear, and now, we're all dead. Well, fuck you."

Alexander took two objects out of his drawer, a pistol, and a bottle. His hands trembled as he poured a shot. Liquor spilled all over the papers atop his desk. The sun would set in two hours.

He committed to performing in Delgado tonight. If he played his cards right, they'd pull off one last show and get some road money and disappear. He'd ditch the Indian and go off into a small town and lie low for a while. He'd made enough money; this one last little taste tonight would be it, the end of the medicine show. He'd change his name and become a banker or live alone. He'd start over fresh from here on out.

He took a few moments with the bottle. Alexander damn well knew this may be his final time enjoying the silence with a shot of whiskey, but he'd never admit it to himself.

Finally, after considering his options, he got up and walked to the door of his little coach, and hollered outside for his two thugs to come inside. Rory and Robert were brothers he'd picked up around the Oregon territory a spell back. Dumb as mules but did what he told them to—no questions asked, and at a fraction of the cost of a man with half an idea in his head.

Alexander briefed his men. He was vague, but explained a man in black might be looking for them as others had in the past over a refund or a pregnancy. He instructed them to take no chances or waste their time with anyone else.

"I ain't even sure he'll show. Just keep your wits bout' you and if you see a man dressed like death, don't ask questions. Start firing. We crystal?"

The two morons nodded and stumbled out of the office with their sloping brows and thick Neanderthal feet. The two Oregon boys were apt at muscling problems off the site or scaring folks into never coming back. They earned their keep while the Indian hung in the darkness and out of sight.

The Indian was capable of worse than anything one could imagine, but he was tricky—some day's you got the killer, and others he wanted nothing to do with any of them. He'd get a wild look in his eyes, and trot off on the back of his Appaloosa somewhere.

Alexander imagined what Charley Warchief exactly did when he left camp for days. He'd turn up when he felt like it, and Alexander wasn't too keen on asking questions. The Comanche would usually show up with supplies or a woman strapped to the back of him. He'd play with the woman in his little wagon cart, but before long he'd leave her body off in a corner of the woods.

Even though they'd known another for many years, Alexander and Charley Warchief never shared a true conversation. Most of the talking was on Alexander's part while the Indian processed the words, offered a nod and moved on. He never disagreed, and when Alexander hatched an idea for outside funding requiring dirty work, the Indian was the man for the job. How they'd managed this partnership so long, was a mystery.

Recently, Warchief strangled an opposing Kiowas behind an outhouse. No rhyme or reason, it was the blood war continuing within him. He had heard a Kiowas lived amongst the white men in a town they passed through.

Out of spite, the Comanche slithered onto his property and waited in the darkness. He cased the scene and made sure he lived alone, or anyone else in the house would die, too. When his blood enemy came outside to take a leak, the Warchief came from behind and pressed his thumbs into his windpipe. The body dropped from the surprise. Charley Warchief slid the piss-stained body behind the defecation shack and walked away.

He didn't loot the house, or steal a horse. He didn't even know the man's name, just that he was his mortal enemy. That was enough.

Phineas Alexander felt as good as a consciously marked man felt. Small noises jarred him from his preparation, while out of the corner of his eye—something moved. His two Oregon meatheads drove the two show coaches to the town square and set up. The little trio playing homey mountain songs hooted and hollered.

They were a cheap and easy way to whet the appetite of the passersby. While the civilians clapped their hands and stomped in the dirt, they were led into the arms of the medicine show. Best of all, the band worked on their commission; Alexander didn't pay them a dime.

The Oregon Boys took their posts at the sides of the wagon. It was boring standing around waiting for nothing. Everyone in this town looked pretty below average—they'd spot some fool in black from a mile away. Alexander hid in his coach, psyching himself up for when he'd make his grand entrance.

Alexander checked his pocket watch. He looked out through his little window and into the crowd. Faces multiplied, and a good thirty people gathered. No one was in black, or even dark colors.

Maybe Delgado wasn't to be his end. It was the final show, so he'd give them every last little inch of his fire and razzmatazz. Alexander opened the door to the outside world and exhaled. He hoped gunfire wouldn't erupt the moment he stepped onto the platform. As he raised his arms, the crowd looked to him, as he stood at the back door of his coach.

The boys stood on either side, bored to tears. Alexander slowly moved to the steps. He smiled wide and fake. The Ghost wasn't coming; he'd deliver a good one tonight. In all of his trepidation, Phineas Alexander overlooked a significant detail: his revolver sat on the desk.

"Brothers and Sisters!" He shouted as his eyes scanned the faces of the townspeople of Delgado.

"I'm here to soothe the soul! I'm here to save your lives. I have the keys to everlasting love and piety. I know the secrets of the sages of savages out in the plains. I've traversed this beautiful land. I've broke bread with many an enlightened soul. I'm here to promise to cure the bugs haunting your aches and pains. I'm Dr. Axlerod, saver of the being, and creator of the world's finest cure all's. Let me explore your mind, body, heart and spirit!"

The audience clapped fierce. A fantastic sign.

The band strummed a ramshackle rendition of Clementine while Alexander pressed the flesh and worked the crowd. His first small sermon/introduction to the show was flawless. He was fiery and potent. They bought the dogshit in spades.

Stunned, small town faces watched as their reflection shined in the toes of his patented leather boots. He felt their money, and it begged him to take it. The energy of the moment added a distinctive pinch of fire usual reserved for the bigger towns.

The Oregon boys stood at their posts watching the perimeter around the coach. Bored, smoking while the fading sun kissed their shirt-sleeved arms.

They were on the lookout for anything odd, and as of yet the only thing out of the ordinary was an old man picking his nose and devouring the green nasal fungi on his finger. They traded yawns and wished they were on a real job out with the crazy Indian.

Both of the boys stood at attention when someone appeared in their sightline. The Oregon boys looked around, making sure they saw the same vision. It was not a mirage. A knockout of a woman; a blonde, buxom showgirl made eyes with each of them; girls never bothered with their sloped brows, and general Neanderthal-like qualities unless they paid for it. No woman ever gave them a second glance.

The woman's painted blue eyes entranced the two young gentlemen, and as she winked, giving breathless coo's, or bit her cherry red lips in devastating, shy sexy style, the brothers went to putty.

Alexander, busy selling seats in heaven, and promising a stellar sermon on "universal truths, a glorious mixture of true tried and true Christian forgiveness mixed with painted, earth alchemy of the original Americans," wasn't paying a lick of attention to the boys.

The Ghost was out of Alexander's mind; he was sure he wouldn't get assassinated in front of these people. The Ghost was a dogfighter, but he, at least, had the decency not to gun a man down in front of women and children. Alexander grew cocky, his swagger flushed over the more he considered the situation with The Ghost on his heels. He'd not shoot him today. There was no way. He'd been acting foolish in there. Once this rat's nest of a town was in dust in the wind, he'd worry about taking cover.

The Oregon boys grew hot under the collar. Their bodies tensed, and their hearts thumped in their chests watching this dame dab her lady parts with a handkerchief. She fanned herself just slightly so. She taunted them. She begged them to do something without saying a word. Her ample assets were on display, and all eyes not focused on the Heavenly Kingdom were on her. She gave a quick few air kisses toward the Oregon Two and called them over with a few curls of her index finger.

Aw shucksing and rubbing their boot toes in the dirt, they lit up scarlet. They'd never seen a woman so perfect beckon their services.

With faces red as apples, they ambled toward the woman. Within seconds, she whispered in their ears. Like firecrackers just before the flame hits the powder, the boys quaked. The platinum-haired whore led her weak little boys off toward her promised land.

Alexander was too mired in meet and greets to notice, and when he did, it was time to get up and make these people love him. He raged. Vulnerable and alone, anything was possible. Where the hell did his employees go, he wondered? There was no sign of The Ghost. He'd heard no gun play and everything pretty quiet.

The oddest thing he saw was the whore dressed for work hanging around for a few seconds, but even then, he couldn't get caught making eyes, it'd ruin him. He'd learned long ago to play the role with the tiniest details, or risk being found out by a stickler.

He didn't panic. There had to be a logical explanation why they'd moved from their positions. They never did anything less than what he demanded. Still, he was without his main two bodyguards, and without his Comanche. Alexander felt alone. Wheeling into his final act, he took a breath and dug in.

"Brothers and Sisters. It's time to repent. The hour has reached us where we need to cure our hearts of poison." He took off his hat and rolled up his shirtsleeves for bravado.

He'd done this so many times. He fell right into character. The people stood ready to see a man save their souls.

"Folks, I know one thing: this here world's hard. When life gets you down, you feel like crawling into a hole and giving up. I've been there a dang many time. But, that ain't the way. Gotta find a light. Somewhere inside of y'all, past a place of misery, and place of hurt is a door to the Kingdom that will break bonds, and shatter fear deep inside.

We here the Magic Medicine & Tribal Spirits believe you'll be able to reach such a place within yourself to fight the inner demons, and hold off on them bad feelings when you wouldn't tell a soul what the end of a gun tasted like, or what a world without his Lord and Savior was like. You need to cherish your soul, and use it to your will to connect with the heavens, like a beacon."

It was total horseshit. Nine times out of ten a pack of yokels like these loved the magical weaving of celebration meets fiery sermon. Being learned wasn't in vogue, so relying on the Unknown was logical. Folks were content with shoveling this trash it into their brains and shutting the lid. The rhetoric grew worse. Alexander jumped and waved a bible, and a bottle of his:

Special priced for *TODAY ONLY* Elixir of Self

He promised them safety. He promised them health. He gave them rainbows and puppy dog tails. He pledged The Kingdom of Heaven.

He begged them that he'd listen to their sorrows and place a healing hand upon the brows of any babe fighting an illness. He was without the power to heal adults through The Lord hadn't granted him such a precious gift. Most of the townspeople didn't question it or him—even though common sense knew small children couldn't talk.

"I was once an evil man. Oh yes, I sinned. I did unspeakable acts I'm ain't proud of." Alexander waived his arms toward God as a man drowning in the seas of glorious light. Those watching were entranced. To them, this moment was defining, and it mattered.

"Today, I stand before you as a man whose soul is clean of transgressions."

Lie.

"I do not lie, philander, steal or lay with woman of ill repute!"

Fable.

"I wouldn't ever turn my back on a friend in need. I am a lover of men, and cast no stones."

Fib.

《《 — 》》

The sun would be gone soon as the colors of the sky were a vicious burnt orange, signifying the day was over. The sun laid its hat on its celestial hook; it was bedtime for the day. The Delgado townspeople would follow suit. He needed to wrap this up. They'd trail off, tired and wanting to return to their lives. Right now it was about the BANG!

He looked around, past the people watching his one-man show, and still no sign of The Ghost, or his Oregon boys. The Ghost wasn't coming; he wouldn't hide. He'd dare him, and he'd taunt him, but he'd never do it right here out in the open.

Alexander's arms went wide like the savior on the cross. He begged for the believers of Delgado to feel the emotion he gave them straight from his soul.

Townspeople hung their heads, and raised their arms to the sky, letting the vibrations of the words sink into them, making the dogma of two cross belief systems blend in them.

"Folks, I'm here to make sure you enter our father's Heavenly home. I've consulted the books of the word of our Lord and met with tribal elders of the native peoples around this great American nation of states.

I've created juice, a potion full of life that'll spark away demonation, and any nefarious intent out of you. The taste is a smooth chicory blend and won't harm your breath. I just know you'll love it."

The show was wrapping up, one more knockout punch and he was home free.

"The Devil takes many forms. Can be a man like you or me. He'll invade the hearts of good men, and strip away the paint of a man's soul if you let him. That there Devil is the bottle of whiskey in your cupboard if you let him rob you of your life. You're my friends here. And friends help friends." He smiled.

"So who wants a bottle?" he said with creamy tone.

Alexander looked defeated from his words scratching out from his soul, but came off like a proud lion, showing he was a servant to the words. Dire, meaningful words that came from within; God's words—they bought it. Again. They cheered and clapped in waves of applause. Some of the things he said he knew didn't make a lick of sense, but the people didn't take much from the message, they wanted the spiritual hand holding of a date with destiny. They wished to be a part of God's Big Show, in whatever forms it took.

The band struck up again. Townspeople lined up to get his special "spirit saving" potion. Everything he had was inside the coach.

Typically, the Oregon boys set up selling area a few moments before he'd wrap up and, he'd walk over, take the money and grasp the hands of anyone suffering.

He'd let them know he was there for them, and he'd be in town for a while to hear their struggles… for a donation to this little traveling church. He promised to pray for them, their children, and all those who suffer.

Phineas Alexander's blood boiled. A vicious streak went through him, and he'd get even with those slimy curs for cutting out on him. He took a bow and promised all who were waiting he'd be returning momentarily with the elixir.

He'd planned to change his shirt then grab the bottles he'd already packaged, and sell what he could. Unless the people wanted to stand around and wait on him, he was behind. He'd lose money, and those two stupid bastards were the reason. He'd kill them when he saw their sad faces. For a moment, he wondered if The Ghost had gotten to them, but that wasn't his style, being sneaky. Turning the knob, he entered the coach. The fading sunlight was at his back as the first thing his eyes settled on were a pair of black boots sitting crossed at the ankles atop his desk.

"Come on in, pookie. Take a load off."

Phineas Alexander's body froze. The Ghost's revolver pointed at him, and he stood unarmed. The band strummed through a crooked rendition of She wore a Yellow Ribbon and outside the people clapped and sang along. The subject matter of the song gave Phineas Alexander chills. It sounded sweet.

'Round her neck she wears a yeller ribbon,
She wears it in winter and the summer so they say,
If you ask her "Why the decoration?"
She'll say "It's fur my lover who is fur, fur away.

Alexander let the door click behind him. The lock exploded into place louder than ever in Alexander's mind. He stepped inward. The Ghost motioned for him to take a seat. The big black preacher's hat cast a long shadow over The Ghost's face, driving fear deeper into Alexander. He so desperately wanted to see the face of his killer.

The Ghost sucked the spit off the front of his top teeth and swallowed. The sound made Alexander uneasy.

"Be rational," Phineas Alexander pleaded.

"What's there to talk about? You knew I was coming." The Ghost held up Holbrook's note for Alexander to see.

"You're probably stumped where your big boys are? Well, I paid this damn fine whore who's sweet as pie to break 'em off a piece. The Funny thing is, you never paid them enough to afford a woman. First chance to get a piece of pussy come— dropped right out. Didn't hafta kill them. I got 'em sexed."

"Walked right up into your coach here while you pressed the flesh. No one said a word. I walked right in, took this seat and listened to the whole thing. Band's good too."

Alexander stared at the laces in his shoes. A cool layer of sweat built up while his stomach was sick with fear of death.

"Can't we be reasonable?" Alexander pleaded. He was trying to get the money in his pockets when The Ghost motioned for him to take it easy, and relax and sit still in his chair.

Alexander tightened his hands together. The sweat between his fingers made his grip greasy. He felt like bawling.

"I'll talk. I'll give you anything you want. I can tell you whatever it is you need to find the others."

"I didn't even start declaring my position, and you're already trying to keep your ass out of a coffin. Ain't happening. The letter told the truth. They're dead." He cocked the hammer. A cold sweat trickled down Phineas Alexander's spine.

"Die like a man, Phineas."

The Ghost fired into Phineas Alexander's head.

The body fell over. Dark blood splattered the money he'd thrown. The Ghost rose from behind the desk. As The Ghost stepped outside, a dozen or so people milled around.

They looked up toward the door, hopeful their savior would come great them and apologize for being gone. They were given nothing. They weren't deaf; they heard the shot.

He tethered the sorrel to the coach and told the band to split.

"Where's your base camp?" The Ghost asked the bandleader, handing him the wad of bloodstained money.

"Up beyond the ridge, past the stream. It's not even two miles. Why do you ask?" The bandleader questioned while rubbing the back of his neck—shy.

"Phineas is dead."

"Oh my God. What happened?" The bandleader was stunned.

"I killed him."

At first, the musician opened his mouth, ready to ask questions, and then sanity took hold. The musician tipped his hat and moved along. The second coach containing the entertainers rode off like a bat out of hell, and no one looked back, never to step foot in Delgado ever again.

CHARLEY WARCHIEF

Darkness spread across the land when The Ghost rode over the hill. Before his eyes raged a massive fire. Many feet wide, at least fifteen feet tall, the smoke drifted far into the night sky. With his back to the inferno, Charley Warchief sat cross-legged, lost in his mind. He was naked to his waist with war paint smeared across his face, chest and clumped in his hair, along with eagle feathers. Charley Warchief remained stoic. He watched The Ghost come down toward him.

The Ghost squinted to check if anyone waited in the darkness. The Indian was unarmed. The sorrel trotted slowly toward the scene. The Ghost was leery of what the Indian planned. He called out. "Charley Warchief!"

The Indian's eyes followed the stars as his neck bobbed up and down, throating a spiritual murmur. His head eased down, and his eyes leveled upon The Ghost. The sorrel sighed, feeling the wave of heat coming from the burning piles of wood.

"I have been waiting for you," he said, over the pops and cracks of the fire.

"That a fact? All this fire for me?"

"It is. I knew you were coming. I am not armed as you can see. Come closer. We will not battle with pistols," Charley Warchief said.

"What if I don't wanna come closer?" The Ghost asked, curious as to why such a storied killer sat without anything to hunt him with.

"My soul is ready. I am ready. I will not face you, a true warrior, without respect. I do not have a weapon."

"I could blow your head clean off."

"You won't. An honorable man doesn't kill because he's mean-hearted, or savage. You kill because you are a lawman of the Heavens. You kill for the right reasons. You are a true warrior. Please drop from your horse." The Indian lifted his hands to show he wasn't hiding anything.

The Ghost dismounted from his horse. His hands dangled near his weapons. Charley Warchief didn't move.

"Sit. We must talk."

"Jesus, I'm talked out."

The Indian blew the comment off. Holding out his hand, he motioned for The Ghost to sit across from him. The fire raged behind the painted man. The flames and darkness overhead gave him a spiritual glow. The Ghost eyeballed the big man sitting across from him. He felt odd going along with the Indian's requests, yet felt at ease and without threat. Still, violence danced in the air.

"I know Phineas is dead. I knew it when I read his face this afternoon. The wind told me the pale horse would ride here tonight, and here you are."

"This's a strange way to meet a man whose rode across the country to kill you."

"You are a warrior. And I cannot disrespect the warrior's blood. You have killed with purpose and reason. I am a killer of men because I hate all. I am no one's friend and no one's ally."

"Why'd you take up with them white boys in The Red Seven? Why didn't you stick with your kind?" The eyes of Charley Warchief weren't menacing or stone cold like they'd been described: they showcased pain. The Ghost saw a vast nothingness; souls swam past trying to escape his gaze.

The Ghost noticed the dead right eye glow gray against the fire. What was there was a man whose community, his lineage was destroyed, and hated the world because of it. He held a hatred for all living men. His people, the Comanches, were warriors taught to fight for their land, to prove their blood was sacred, and they were the greatest of all tribes. With the firepower and cunning of the white men who shot them full of holes, the whites found ingenious ways to murder a once proud people. Charley Warchief was a man without a home.

Because he wasn't a snapping, snarling beast who killed him instantly, it didn't mean he wasn't dangerous. If anything, the pause in action proved he was methodical and as maniacal as rumored.

"I rode with the white man because they were men of nothing."

Charley Warchief rose. His hands were massive, as was the girth of his body. He was three of The Ghost. The Ghost pulled his revolver and aimed it at the Indian.

"No. I will not die by your machine. No more guns." He spat on the ground.

The Ghost was confused at what was happening. Charley Warchief knew he was coming and didn't arm himself. He didn't move when a gun was pulled on him and didn't lunge at The Ghost at any moment. He didn't kneel down to be tapped on the back of the head with a shot to get it over, either.

"I want you to fight me. The spirit of the bear is in me. A warrior's death. You are the last of the men who fear nothing. You hunted me, and I want the hunter to kill his prey like the animal he is."

The Ghost aimed his gun at Charley Warchief and pulled the trigger. The giant Indian was fast for his size. The shot missed. Before The Ghost pulled off his second rapid fire shot with the heel of his hand, the Indian's shoulder was crashing into him, knocking him to the ground. The Indian took the revolver and opened it, letting the bullets fall to the dirt. He ripped the second revolver out of the place in The Ghost's belt and tossed it into the darkness.

The Indian growled like a wild animal and gave praise to the moon hanging above. The Ghost returned to his feet and wiped the blood coming from his mouth. The shotgun was mounted on the sorrel. Warchief stood closer.

"You are unarmed. Fight me and let one of us rise to the spirits and find our place with the old Gods." His voice boomed as he crouched over, ready to fight. His fingers looked like long talons, ready to sink into The Ghost's flesh.

The Ghost's eyes never left the Warchief. He took off his shirt and hat. His boots came next. Both men circled one another: two snapping dogs against the firelight. The Ghost lunged forward, the image of his family's head's on pikes at the forefront of his mind. Suffering and pain drove him. Blood in, blood out.

The Ghost stepped forward and moved inward, toward the midsection of the larger man taking a powerful swing. The Warchief sidestepped him again and landed a direct shot to the side of The Ghost's neck below the left ear.

The Ghost dropped to the earth's floor. Pain shot through

his body. His fingers clutched the dirt below as raucous laughter came from above.

"You are nothing without a gun. Get up and show me why so many men fear you when they hear your name. I murdered your family.

The Ghost rose.

The Ghost screamed as he swung his fists at a furious speed, hoping to land at least a few of the blows. Charley Warchief blocked the shot at his face. The Ghost's right connected with his stomach at the right angle of breath and the air leapt out of the big Indian. The Ghost followed with a direct clip to the jaw.

Charley Warchief staggered but didn't fall. He growled again through his teeth and spat blood as he threw a punch into The Ghost's mouth. The rate and speed of the slug sent a tooth flying from The Ghost's mouth. He'd lost an upper.

The two men grabbed one another in a vicious bear-hugging match as their sweating, shirtless bodies twisted into one. As arms squeezed, and hands slapped against flesh, they cursed and damned one another while the flames behind them feasted upon the wood.

The Ghost broke free from Charley Warchief's grip on his neck and landed an elbow to the throat at the perfect angle. He spun a fist and connected it to the Indian's ear. The Indian spat a mouthful of blood into The Ghost's face.

Shrieking, he landed a kick in the center of The Ghost's thigh. The Ghost saw the revolver laying there and grabbed it by the barrel. He struck the butt of the gun over Charley Warchief's head, splitting a patch of flesh open. The crazy bastard howled like a wolf between psychotic fits of laughter. His knees buckled, yet the man didn't fall.

Blood, dirt, greasepaint and sweat all intermixed on his skin. The Ghost's teeth showed. He was possessed like a rabies-infected dog looking to sink his teeth into his enemy.

He took another swing with the end of the revolver, hoping one more blow would put this massive creature from hell down, even while bleeding and hurt, Charley Warchief knocked the gun free from The Ghost's grip.

Warchief wrapped his large hand around The Ghost's neck and squeezed. The air stopped flowing. He felt his heart pounding harder as the pressure was applied to his Adam's apple. The Ghost took a swing from his heels and connected to the face of Charley and in return, Charley nailed him good in the chops. Falling forwards for a second, The Ghost found his footing, and lunged forward, driving a knee into the ribcage of the Indian. He took a hold of the blood-soaked, filthy black mane and slammed his knee into the face of his aggressor.

The Ghost imagined he was freeing the people who died by this man's hands. Through the ultra violence, the Indian dared him to come out of his soul.

"Show me to the grave. Take me to the underworld where I belong. Do your worst." A layer of blood was atop the smiling Charley Warchief's lips and teeth. His stance was shaky but solid. He beckoned and dared The Ghost to make his move. His body bobbed and weaved like a boxer.

The Ghost moved forward and tried to kick Warchief's feet out from under him. His bootless foot connected with ankles of the warrior. The Indian grabbed The Ghost by the hair and smashed his fist into the facial cavity. Stars erupted behind his eyes as the massive, forceful fist ripped his lips, nose and skin to shreds with rough knuckles. His scalp hurt from the fingers gripping his hair and pulling upward. With both fists together like a club, The Ghost swung hard and landed a shot in the chest of Warchief.

The force of the hit sent the Indian back a foot, allowing The Ghost to regain his stance, despite the swirling universe around his head.

They stopped to size one another up; their hearts thundered in their chests. In silent agreement, The Ghost and Charley Warchief ran full speed at one another. The sweat and blood drifted off their aching bodies and through the air like silken sashes of suffering.

The Ghost leveled what strength remained from his heels up to the tips of his fingers. The uppercut landed square on the jaw. Charley Warchief's teeth sunk into his tongue, severing the meat. The Warchief was brought off his toes. His body landed into the dirt below. The Ghost raced for the shotgun. When Charley Warchief sat up, a trail of blood ran from his mouth down across his chest.

Their eyes met.

"You don't deserve a warrior's death. You deserve the death of a piece of shit for killing innocents. Enjoy whatever fucking hell you go to."

The Ghost squeezed the trigger of the shotgun. The body fell face first into the dirt. The blood soaked into the dirt around the Indian. The Ghost caught his breath.

Blood was caked on his face. He pushed his sweaty hair from his eyes. For the first time in his life, The Ghost was scared. He came close to dying many times before; only nothing was as carnal, bestial as this.

He struggled to stop his body from shaking and wiped his

nose and mouth dry with the back of his disgusting arm.

He coughed and wiped the tears from his eyes. He tasted a death so salacious, so lucid—it was too real.

He'd cheated the grim reaper once again.

EPILOGUE

Charley Warchief's body lay in the flame of the fire. The kiss of the burn stripped the viciousness away as he was free from the chains of hatred. The Ghost, broken and bruised, mounted up and headed over the hills toward his future. He hoped Annabelle and Simon would be there waiting for him. The only thing between him and love was the expanse of the American wilderness.

As they reached the top of the hill, the fire crept higher into the night sky. Birds sat quietly in trees while the stars hung hazy overhead. Bad men did horrific things in every town across the globe, and there'd never be a shortage of bounties. Since the dawn of time, men have killed one another for nothing, but for this moment, all sat right with the world. The Ghost enjoyed the silence and knew his brother, Mattie, and the kids were at peace.

He'd plant a big garden to remember them; the vibrant colors of the flora would signify the wonder of life, but act as a reminder that despite the terrible things mankind was capable of, there would always be redemption.

The Ghost clicked his reigns and directed the horse to its new home. It was time to rest.

No more bullets.

No more guns.

No more suffering.

For as long as men carried bleakness within their hearts, there would always be evil in the world. For this moment, he enjoyed the silence of the calming fires, because tomorrow was a new day. He didn't believe in rebirth, but reality, and there would always be a grave to fill. He didn't want to spoil such the moment with such grim thoughts.

ROBERT DEAN is a New Orleanian living in Austin exile. You can find his books in bookstores and on Amazon. You can find him all over the Internet, bitching about something. Currently, he's hard at work on a new novel and poetry collection.

His fucked up memoir about living in New Orleans is still seeking a home. He also likes ice cream and panda bears.

@Robert_Dean
facebook.com/robertdeansworld

81828139R00115

MadeMade in the USA
Columbia, SC
11 December 2017